The Ultimate Pi Day Party

Baldwin Village, Book 1

Jackie Lau

First edition: March 2019
ISBN: 978-1-7753047-9-1

Editor: Latoya C. Smith, LCS Literary Services

Cover Design: Flirtation Designs

Cover photograph: Shutterstock

For Dad

"WILL YOU MARRY ME?"

Amrita is down on one knee in front of me, holding a ring box and a single rose. She's wearing a spiffy black suit with a white shirt and red bow tie.

"My first proposal." I lean back against my desk. "I don't know what to say."

"Say you'll marry me. Or are you going to make me beg?"

"Hmm. I kind of want to see you beg."

She smacks my leg. "Come on."

"Yes, I'll marry you."

She stands up and gives me a quick hug before stepping back. "Now tell me what you think. The suit, the rose—is it okay?"

There's a touch of uncertainty in her voice, which isn't like Amrita. My best friend usually exudes confidence.

"It's more than okay," I say. "Except your bow tie's a little crooked." I move to straighten it, but she slaps my hand away.

"It's supposed to be crooked. It's *jaunty*."

"Right. A *jaunty* bow tie."

"You're making fun of me."

"I'm not. It's nice." I gesture at her suit. "I can't believe you're getting engaged."

"She still has to say yes."

"Holly will say yes. You know that."

Amrita grins at me.

Two years ago, I never would have imagined her standing in my office with a rose and a ring, preparing to propose to someone. If I'd mentioned the idea to her, she would have wrinkled her nose and laughed in my face. But she's been with Holly for a while now, and here we are.

Her phone rings.

"Just a sec, this won't be long," she says, then answers the call and begins speaking rapidly in Punjabi. I take a seat behind my desk and wait for her to finish.

I've known Amrita since university, and we started Hazelnut Tech together several years ago. I'm the CEO, and she's the CTO. We have an office just east of Yonge Street in downtown Toronto, as well as offices in Montreal and Vancouver.

Amrita ends the call. "My mom wanted to know whether I'd proposed yet."

My eyes widen. "I can't believe you told her you were going to propose."

"I can't believe it, either. It just slipped out when I saw her last weekend." Once upon a time, Amrita's parents were not supportive of the fact that she likes women, but they've come around. "She also says that she's found a nice woman for you, Josh."

I cough. "What?"

"You heard me. My mother wants to set you up with someone."

"I hope you said no."

She shrugs.

"Amrita!"

"Okay, fine. I said no, but the thought of her bringing this woman to the office? It was tempting."

I glare at her. "You wouldn't dare."

"Maybe I would, but tonight is not the night for me to think about your poor excuse for a love life." She tugs the lapels of her suit jacket, then uses her phone as a mirror to fix her short hair.

I ignore her comment about my love life. I don't have one... because I don't want one. Besides, I'm too busy with work for a relationship. I do, however, have a sex life, although I've had a bit of a dry spell lately.

I push that thought aside. "February thirteenth is an odd day to propose."

"Exactly! That's the point. It'll be a surprise. Valentine's Day is too obvious, but the day *before* Valentine's? She won't be expecting it."

"Right."

"Come on, Josh. Sound happy for me."

"I *am* happy. I just..." I don't know. I've been in a bit of a funk lately, and it's Valentine's Day tomorrow, and I've had to see red roses and hearts *everywhere*.

"It's okay," she says. "I'll see you on Friday?"

"Friday?" It's only Wednesday. "Why not tomorrow?"

She gives me a look. "I told you about my plan to take Valentine's Day off, remember? Unless Holly says no, and then—"

"She'll say yes, don't worry. And you look good. Really, you do."

Amrita gives me a smile, then leaves my office.

I walk to the window and look out at the street below. It's snowing today. Not much, but even a little snow can mess up traffic. There's a bunch of honking, and some idiot is driving too quickly down the crowded, snowy streets.

I head back to my desk. Time to answer some emails, but my head isn't in the game.

Instead, I pick up the picture of my family that's gathering dust on the shelf beside my desk. Dad, Mom, me, and my sisters, Nancy and Wendy, at Nancy's wedding several years ago. Dad isn't smiling. He rarely smiles in photos, especially not when he's forced to stand beside his only son. Amrita's office is decorated with pictures of Holly, but me, on the other hand…I only have this one dusty photo of my family.

I turn it over and sigh.

~

When I leave the office, it's dark. I don't feel like heading home and cooking, so I wander north from Hazelnut Tech, planning to grab something to eat before I get on the subway.

I pass Chinese restaurants, ramen restaurants, a falafel place. A British pub next to an Indian restaurant, which is next to a Korean barbecue restaurant.

Nothing appeals, however.

I consider going to a Hong Kong-style café I like, but I'm not in the mood.

I'm not in the mood for anything.

Why do I feel like this? Am I annoyed that my best friend is getting engaged? It's not like I'm jealous—I don't want what she has for myself. But I also don't think she's making a mistake. She and Holly will be very happy together.

I find myself in Baldwin Village, a small section of Baldwin Street east of Chinatown where the houses have been converted to businesses. Mostly restaurants, many with patios out front, gathering snow in the dead of February. Pupusa Hut, Paulie's Laksa, Hogtown Poke, Elk Bistro…

And then I see a place that makes me smile.

Happy As Pie.

The name of the shop sounds vaguely familiar, though I can't place it.

But pie sounds like the perfect dinner. A slice of lemon

meringue, a slice of apple pie, and a cup of coffee—that should hit the spot.

I step inside, glad to be out of the bitter cold, and peruse the offerings. I'd expected it to just serve sweet pies, but there are savory ones, too. It appears I'll be able to have a proper meal after all, rather than just a big dessert.

There are four meat pies: tourtière, braised lamb and rosemary, beef and mushroom, and chicken and leek. No one's behind the counter, though, and I'm the only customer.

"Hello?" I call. There's a door—presumably to the kitchen—that's open just a crack.

It opens further, and a white woman with a big smile and light brown hair steps out. She's about my age, and she's wearing an apron over her nicely-shaped—

Never mind. I'm here for pie, not to ogle some woman's figure.

"What can I get you?" she asks. She has a lovely voice. Soft, but not too quiet, and musical, somehow.

"I'll have a beef and mushroom pie," I say.

"Sure thing."

"And a coffee."

"Alright."

"A slice of pear ginger crumble pie."

"Yep."

"And a butter tart. All for here."

She raises her eyebrows. "Will that be everything? Are you sure you don't also want a slice of cherry pie and a slice of chocolate tart?"

I smile, enjoying her teasing. "No, that's all."

I pay for the large meal, and she says she'll bring it over to me. I go to sit by the window and watch the snow fall on the empty patio.

My phone buzzes. It's Amrita.

She said yes!

Congrats, I reply, then set my phone aside.

The woman sets a warm beef and mushroom pie in front of me, followed by a second plate with my desserts.

"Enjoy," she says.

"I'm sure I will, thank you." And then it comes to me. I remember where I've heard of this pie shop. "Last month, the premier got hit in the face with a pie at Queen's Park."

She sighs. "Yes, that was one of our pies."

"A cherry pie, if I remember correctly?"

"No, it was a special order for a banana cream pie with lots of whipped cream."

"Much less colorful."

That gets a smile out of her, and her smile is a thing of beauty.

"I had no idea what they were going to use it for," she says. "If it wasn't going to be eaten, why didn't they just buy a pie from the grocery store and add whipped topping from a can?"

I chuckle. "You tired of hearing about it?"

"I always hoped that when we got some press, it would be for how great the pies taste, not for how they look when smashed on a politician's face."

"Yeah, I can imagine."

"Though his political rivals did place an order for six banana cream pies, extra whipped cream, so it's not like I didn't get any business out of it. I shouldn't complain."

"I'm sure you'll get the business you want soon enough."

"Thank you."

She smiles at me before walking away, and I try the pie. The beef and mushroom is delicious. The crust is flaky, and the filling is rich and steaming. Perfect for a chilly winter's day.

I have stuff to do. A proposal for an app for a food delivery service to review. Too many emails in my inbox. But instead I just sit here, enjoying my pie.

I sip my coffee, then move on to dessert, starting with the butter tart. It's a high-quality butter tart, and I consider myself a connoisseur. Although I feel disloyal to even think it, it's better—just a teeny-tiny bit better—than my mother's butter tarts.

My mother worked as a cook at a Chinese-Canadian buffet in Ottawa. She was responsible for the so-called Canadian food, which included roast beef and mashed potatoes. She also made apple pie and butter tarts, a Canadian specialty with filling that's a bit like pecan pie without the pecans. Butter, syrup, sugar, and egg, if I remember correctly. She taught me to make them when I was ten.

I think that's why I was tempted by the pie shop: it reminds me of those last happy days with my parents, before my mom got sick. Before I went on my rebellious teenage streak, culminating with the unfortunate incident that caused my father to quit talking to me.

My mom is better now, and my parents are both retired, but my dad still hasn't forgiven me, and he refuses to come to Toronto for a visit.

Yet despite the fact that he's essentially forgotten I exist, I think of him every day. I can't help but hope that one day, I will be enough for him. My mother and I get along okay, but my dad is a different matter.

I put down the butter tart and pick up a forkful of the pear ginger crumble pie. Oh my God, it's exquisite. It's quite gingery—I love ginger—and the crumble topping is perfect.

Seriously, this might be the best thing I've ever eaten in my life.

"Did you make this?" I ask the woman in the apron, gesturing at the pear pie.

"No, but they're all my recipes. Except for the famous banana cream pie. That one's my mom's."

Suddenly, I imagine my own mother meeting this woman, swapping pie recipes with her.

What the fuck is wrong with me?

I don't want the kind of relationship with a woman that

would involve her meeting my *mother*. And I don't know this woman. I don't even know her name.

It must be because of Amrita and Holly's engagement. That has to be why I'm having these weird thoughts.

I savor the rest of my pie. I wish there were more, but I've already eaten a lot tonight, and I should probably restrain myself from getting another piece.

I take my dishes up to the counter, and I'm about to head out when the woman says, "You have something on your lip." She points to the left corner of her lip. "Butter tart filling."

I swipe at the left corner of my mouth. I don't feel anything.

"No, I mean, your right side. Which is on my left." She picks up a napkin. "May I?"

I nod, and she wipes off the offending crumb. I feel the warmth of her fingers, just for a moment, and then it's gone.

But for the rest of the evening, I keep touching the corner of my mouth, remembering the feel of her fingers on my skin.

That night, I dream I'm wearing a suit and a crooked—a *jaunty*—red bow tie like Amrita, and I'm down on one knee, holding open a ring box.

I'm proposing to a large pear ginger crumble pie.

I have no idea what the hell that's supposed to mean.

I DON'T USUALLY GET into work at five thirty in the morning, but today is a special day.

It's Valentine's Day.

Not that I have any romantic plans. I haven't been on a date in ages.

But Valentine's Day means that there are several special orders at Happy As Pie, my sweet and savory pie shop in Baldwin Village.

Pie isn't the sort of food that comes to mind when you think of Valentine's Day. However, I have twelve special orders for today. It's nowhere near as much as Thanksgiving weekend, but it's extra business all the same. I'm glad that some people are a little more creative than simply purchasing a box of chocolates.

Even if I have no man waiting for me when I finally get off work in...fourteen hours or so, today is a good day. Sure, it's early, but I've got a cup of coffee and I'm all alone in the kitchen.

I turn on the music and pull out the pumpkin purée, eggs, and cream. First order of business: four pumpkin pies.

Yes, I have multiple orders of pumpkin pie for Valentine's Day. Some people really love their pumpkin pie, and they don't like having to wait until Thanksgiving for it. I sell pumpkin pie in my shop all year round, on Tuesdays, Fridays, and Sundays.

One of these lucky pumpkin pies is even going to witness a proposal. In fact, the man who placed the order wanted me to bake an engagement ring into the pie, but I refused. First of all, I don't want the responsibility of keeping track of a diamond ring, and second of all, I have some unfortunate memories of inedible objects that were baked into desserts.

You see, money cakes were a tradition in my family. For every birthday, my grandmother would bake coins in the cake, and it was always very exciting.

Unfortunately, I swallowed a dime on my eighth birthday, and I totally freaked out. My mom assured me that it would likely pass out the other end, no need to worry, but for two days, I was convinced I would die, no matter how much she reassured me.

Swallowing a dime is one thing, but what if someone swallowed a ten-thousand-dollar engagement ring?

I shudder to think of it.

Nope, no inedible objects are being baked into any of my pies. That's one of my rules.

Anyway, for Valentine's Day orders I'm also making two chocolate tarts, one spiced apple pie, one key lime pie, two lemon meringue pies, and one pear ginger crumble pie. And fifteen butter tarts, for the man who's proposing using butter tarts because they're his girlfriend's favorite.

All this talk of love and engagements makes me think of what I do not have, and I feel a strange ball of tension in my stomach.

I'm thirty-one years old, and I've never had a boyfriend, not unless you count the two weeks I was Jamie Metcalf's girlfriend back in grade three, or the three weeks I was with Daniel Spiers in grade ten. I don't think those really count, though.

Not that there haven't been men, but never anything serious. It was never my priority. My priority was getting the hell out of Ingleford, my tiny hometown where there is absolutely nothing to do, moving to the city, and opening my bakery. At first I thought I wanted a French pâtisserie, but later on, I changed my mind.

And now I have my very own pie shop. It's been open for nearly a year, and I have six employees—pie-making is a rather labor-intensive business. Usually there are three or four of us in the kitchen, but I always get in an hour early so I can have a little time to myself and sing along with my music.

I wouldn't dare subject anyone else to my off-tune singing.

Really, it's that bad.

I take four pie crusts—frozen in pie pans—out of the freezer. We don't make pie crust every day; instead, we make big batches of pie crust using our large mixer, then have an assembly line of sorts. Once the dough is mixed, one person measures (235 g per pie for our dessert pies), one person rolls, and the third person puts it in the pan and pinches it. Certain types of pies, like pumpkin, are best when the crust is pre-baked so they don't get soggy, so I have to blind bake the crusts before I pour in the filling.

Once the pumpkin pies are in the oven, I start on the key lime pie. This one's a little different, as I use a graham cracker crust. Dylan and Fatima come in when I'm measuring out the apple pie filling, which I made yesterday, for the specially-ordered apple pie, as well as a few for our shop.

"How long have you been here?" Dylan asks. He's a young guy who recently finished college and has yet to become acquainted with haircuts.

"More than an hour," I reply.

"Maybe you should try sleeping one of these days."

I shrug. "I'll take it under consideration."

My job is my life, though, and I love it.

Even if I'm best known for supplying the banana cream pie that ended up on the premier's face.

~

At three in the afternoon, I'm in the kitchen, making pear-ginger filling, when Ann comes to get me.

"There's a couple here. They want to order some pies for their wedding."

I wash my hands and come out to the front, where I introduce myself to a young Asian couple. They're about my age, and they're smiling and holding hands. The guy looks vaguely familiar—I think he might have come into Happy As Pie a few times before? He introduces himself as Wes, and his fiancée is Caitlin. I lead them to a table by the window, a list of all our pies in my hand.

"We're getting married in August," Caitlin says. "We thought about having a wedding cake, but they're usually more about the appearance than taste. Since I really love pie, Wes suggested we have a pie buffet for dessert."

"How many people?" I ask.

"A hundred and fifty. I was thinking thirty pies? Price isn't a concern, and I want there to be lots."

Thirty pies would be my biggest order yet.

Can we do it? Absolutely.

I want to start doing more orders and hopefully get into catering. The focus would be the meat pies, though. There are some companies—mostly tech companies, I think—that provide lunches for their employees every day, or maybe for special occasions, and that would be great business.

Eventually, I'd like to sell frozen meat pies to grocery stores, but that would require Happy As Pie to be a bigger operation than it currently is. Our kitchen isn't huge. A second location, perhaps?

Yes, I have plans.

But first things first. A pie buffet for a wedding...which sounds fantastic, though I'm admittedly biased toward pie.

I slide over the list of pies. "These are all the pies we make regularly."

"Awesome," Wes says. "This looks great."

"We'll definitely get a few key lime pies," Caitlin says. "That's my favorite. Wes bought me a slice from here a couple times."

"No key lime today, but would you like to try a slice or two of something else while you're here?" I stand up. "On the house. Right now, we have spiced apple, cherry, berry crumble, lemon meringue, and chocolate tart."

"I'll have cherry," she says.

"Lemon meringue for me."

I get them their slices of pie, and Caitlin sighs in bliss at her first bite of cherry pie, which makes me smile.

"Oh my God. You need to try this," she says to her fiancé. She holds a forkful of cherry pie to his lips, and he feeds her a bite of lemon meringue pie.

"You've got something on your lip." He wipes it off as he looks at her with utter adoration, then plants a kiss on her lips.

I turn away, hit with a bolt of longing.

And I can't help remembering the man who came into Happy As Pie last night. I didn't know him at all, yet I wiped butter tart filling off his lip. I should have told him to go to the washroom and look in the mirror; I shouldn't go around touching customers, even if I ask them first. I don't know why I acted the way I did.

Okay, maybe I do.

Because he was really fucking handsome, and I spend at least twelve hours a day working, and I don't have a life.

This is what you want, I remind myself.

Yes, I'm living my dream. My mother didn't think I could do it. She thought I should stay in Ingleford, get married, have kids, maybe work as an accountant.

I had other ideas.

And here I am.

I went to college for baking and pastry arts, then spent years working in kitchens at bakeries and cafés, saving money and honing my craft, until I opened my shop nearly a year ago. I sunk everything I had into this. It has to remain my focus. I don't have time for a man, not now.

But today is my first Valentine's Day in my own pie shop, and I'm baking pies for people in love, for people who want to propose, and there's a happy couple feeding each other lemon meringue and cherry pie by the window.

"We'll email you when we decide on the pies," Caitlin says, standing up. "Sometime in the next few days. Would you be able to deliver them to the venue? It's not far from here."

"Sure," I say. We've never delivered anything before, but this is exactly the sort of thing I want to be doing.

Caitlin and Wes leave, and I head back to the kitchen with a smile on my face.

~

I don't get home until eight o'clock that night, after spending fourteen hours at work. Longer than usual, but not every day is Valentine's Day. I live in a small apartment building about a ten-minute walk from Happy As Pie. It's a pretty crappy apartment, to be honest, but it's nearby and I don't spend much time here anyway.

I collapse face-first on my couch for a few minutes, then get up and make myself an omelette and salad for dinner. I eye the two bottles of wine in my cupboard.

Why not? It's Valentine's Day, and I'm alone.

I eat my dinner and drink a glass of sauvignon blanc while sitting at my tiny table and updating our social media accounts. When I'm done, I pull my legs up onto the chair and wrap my arms around them, resting my chin on my knees.

Dammit, I feel pathetic. I shouldn't, but I do.

You know what would be nice? Having a group of good friends. Other single women who could sit around and share a bottle of wine with me on Valentine's Day. Maybe meet me for dinner every week or two. Occasionally send me silly text messages. I never made close friends when I moved to Toronto for college. I was hyper-focused on my dream.

Hmm. Where would I find a friend?

I shake my head and pour myself another glass of wine, and then my mind wanders back to the Asian guy who came into Happy As Pie, to his enticing lips, his smile, the curve of his back. He was maybe five-ten, wearing jeans and a Henley, nothing fancy. Yet he carried himself as though he was someone a little important and could move through the world with ease. He had a nice smile, and I've always been a sucker for a nice smile, plus that shirt hinted at great arm muscles.

I can't say I'm thinking of him as a *friend*.

Sure, there are lots of attractive men in the world, but he was the hottest guy I'd seen in a long time, plus there was just something special about him, aside from his good looks.

I'll probably never see him again, and I can't help feeling more than a little disappointed.

I CAN'T BELIEVE IT. The unthinkable happened.

My father has gotten a Facebook account.

My sister Nancy sent me a text to notify me of this strange development. She'd been shocked when she got a friend request from him.

I didn't get a friend request, though.

Not surprising.

Still, I feel a twinge of *something* at the rejection.

My father is a sixty-five-year-old retired high school math teacher. He doesn't believe in social media and smartphones. He thinks they're a waste of time and rants about how they're destroying society.

Yeah, if I was trying to impress my father, starting a tech company that does a lot of app development wasn't the best way to go, but that's where I saw an opportunity.

Anyway, I've had a Facebook account since it was called "The Facebook" and only available to university and college students. You had to wait for them to add your school. I never thought I'd see the day when my father would be on it.

Not that I spend much time on Facebook, but I go there now

and find my father's profile. He's managed to put up a profile picture in which he's actually smiling, rather than looking like he's constipated or eating a lemon.

I scroll down his profile and see a cartoon with an *i* and a π. There's a speech bubble above each.

"Be rational," says i.

"Get real," says π.

A classic math joke. Since I have a degree in computer science, I'm rather familiar with math jokes. I've seen this particular one on T-shirts.

His next post is another graphic with a math joke. *Don't drink and derive.*

Yeah, I know that one, too.

And the jokes keep going and going.

Did you hear about the mathematician who was afraid of negative numbers? He would stop at nothing to avoid them.

I groan.

What do you call a snake that's 3.14 meters long?

A pi-thon.

I groan again. That's one I haven't heard before.

Apparently, my father has been on Facebook for a while, even though he just friended Nancy, and I see some of his former students commenting on his posts.

My dad was fairly well-liked as a teacher, and he had a reputation for his painful sense of humor and bad puns. His "dad jokes" embarrassed me greatly when I was little, but now that he doesn't talk to me anymore, seeing them makes me smile, even as I groan.

I miss my father. I miss him a lot.

Goddammit.

Okay, I need a break. I've got an important meeting with a prospective client in two hours, and I have to be in the right frame of mind for that.

"I'm going out for a long lunch," I tell Clarissa, my assistant.

"You've got a meeting—"

"I know. I'll be back for that, don't worry."

It's Friday now, and Wednesday's snow is turning gray and crusty along the side of the road. The intersections are a bit slushy. I walk to the sushi restaurant I like, only three blocks away, but when I get there, I'm not in the mood for sushi.

No, for some reason I'm craving pie.

I speed-walk to Happy As Pie, excited to eat some pie...and to see the woman who works there, if I'm honest with myself. She's popped into my mind regularly over the past couple days.

As soon as I get inside, the aroma of apple pie envelopes me, and I start to feel more at ease. The woman behind the counter smiles at me, but it's not the same woman who was working when I was here two days ago. This one is older, maybe forty-five, and her dark hair is scraped into a bun.

I'm disappointed, I admit, but I'm still getting some pie.

"I'll have a braised lamb and rosemary pie," I say, "and a slice of chocolate tart. For here." Alas, there's no pear ginger crumble pie today, but the chocolate tart looks tasty. "And a coffee, too, but you'd better make that to go, just in case." I don't want to be late for my meeting.

Five minutes later, I'm digging into my braised lamb pie, and it is, indeed, amazing. I wolf it down, then start on the chocolate tart. It's delicious, too. Actually, my mother used to make something similar. It was my father's favorite, and she always made it on his birthday.

That's probably why I ordered the chocolate tart. Because I was thinking of my father.

Seventeen years ago, I disappointed him. I disappointed him greatly.

But I have a good life now. My company is doing well, and I own a house in Forest Hill. I recently appeared in a "20 Young Canadian Entrepreneurs to Watch" article, as well as on a list of the "35 Most Eligible Bachelors Under 35 in Toronto."

I forwarded the first one to my mother and the second one to my sisters, which I am now regretting, as they keep teasing me about it

The list actually got quite a bit of press. About half the men on the list were non-white, and some people complained that the magazine was trying too hard to be "politically correct," and "everyone knows Asian men aren't popular with the ladies," etc. Toronto is about fifty percent visible minority, so the numbers were just proportional to the population, but...yeah. That was interesting.

Amrita framed a copy of the list and the little blurb and head-shot of me. She hung it on the wall in my office. I keep taking it down, and she keeps putting it back up.

Most people think I'm doing pretty well in life, with the exception of my dad. I keep thinking that if I could just convince him to come to Toronto from Ottawa and see the Hazelnut Tech office, as well as my house, maybe he'd change his mind. I also want my mother to visit me, but she refuses to come without my dad.

As I stare at my half-finished slice of chocolate tart, I have a brainwave. I know exactly how to get my dad to come to Toronto.

A Pi Day party.

My math teacher father loves Pi Day. Unfortunately for him, it usually fell during March Break, but he always made the first day back from March Break a Pi Day celebration. My mother would make apple pies for all of his classes. Everyone would get a slice of pie, and there would be a special lesson for the day that involved pi. The specifics varied depending on which class it was.

That's what I'll do. I'll throw a Pi Day party for all of my employees, with lots of pie and nerdy jokes, and I'll invite my parents. They can see my house, see all the people I have working at my company.

It's a brilliant plan.

I walk up to the counter. "Do you do catering?" I ask the woman working there.

"Just a moment. Let me get Sarah."

She goes into the back, and a minute later, another woman emerges. The woman who was here on Wednesday night.

Damn, she's pretty. I'd forgotten just how pretty she is.

When she sees me, her lips part, and I remember how she touched *my* lips. A sizzle of heat runs through me.

Yes, this is a particularly brilliant plan if I get to spend more time with *her*.

Wiping her hands on her apron, she says, "Ann tells me you're interested in catering. What sort of event is this for?"

"I want to throw the ultimate Pi Day party."

I NEVER THOUGHT I'd see him again, but here he is, in my shop, talking about Pi Day.

I can't help it. I burst into laughter.

"You want to throw the ultimate Pi Day party," I say slowly.

He tilts his head to the side and smiles at me. "Yes, and I want you to supply the pies." He sticks out his hand. "I'm Josh Yu, CEO of Hazelnut Tech."

I shake his hand, in a bit of a daze. "I'm..." Oh, God, what's my name again? "I'm...Sarah Winters. The owner."

He lets go of my hand, but my hand is still frozen in mid-air.

Apparently, when I shake hands with a really handsome man, I lose control of my limbs.

Once again, he's wearing a Henley. For a moment, I imagine we're on a date, and maybe he'll stroke my thigh or hold my hand under the table, and then after dinner...

Focus, Sarah.

"Tell me a bit about this party," I say, pulling my arm back to my side. "Where will it be? How many people?"

"I have sixty-five employees in Toronto, and if they bring

their partners and families...I don't know. Maybe a hundred and twenty?"

"No problem."

I'm a little intimidated, to be honest, but I don't let on. In the many jobs I've had over the years, I've worked at events that were this big—and much larger. But I've never done anything like this with Happy As Pie.

However, there's no way I'm turning it down, and not only because this gorgeous man is like sex on a stick.

No, this is exactly the sort of opportunity I want, and maybe it'll lead to more things. Perhaps Hazelnut Tech is one of those companies that provides lunches for their employees. If we could do something like that semi-regularly, that would be great. Plus, it'll help to get us known for something other than supplying cream pies to throw at politicians.

My brain is bouncing between thinking like the sensible business owner I always strive to be and being overwhelmed by his attractiveness.

"The party will be at my house," Josh says.

"I hope you have a big house."

He gives me a crooked smile. "It's not bad."

"Rosedale?"

"Forest Hill," he says, naming a wealthy midtown neighborhood.

Ah, okay. This guy and I totally do not run in the same circles. Yet he's personally asked *me* to cater his party.

I can't help the thrill that runs through me.

"Out of curiosity," I say, "how much oven space do you have?"

"Um, the usual amount?"

The meat pies retain heat quite well, and we can probably fit a hundred and twenty into our two ovens, then bring them over already warmed. I expect that's what we'll do, but I want to know my options.

I head to the back, then return with a list of our pies. "I was envisioning meat pies—and vegetable or chickpea ones for the vegetarians—for the main course, then lots of dessert pies. Is that what you had in mind?"

He nods. "Though I confess, I'm not really the party-planning type. Usually my assistant figures out these kinds of things, but this time..." He glances out the window, and the smile slips off his face. "This one is different."

Okay. I wait a beat in case he wants to elaborate, but he doesn't, so I hand over the list. "Here's what I can make, though if there's something else you want, just let me know, and I'll see what I can do."

"Hmm." He reads through the list. "Anything with hazelnuts?"

What the...? It's such an odd request.

And then I remember the name of his company.

"No, nothing with hazelnuts, but..." I think as quickly as I can. "But I could try an apple hazelnut crumble pie? Or something with chocolate."

He snaps his fingers. "Nutella. I want you to make me some kind of Nutella pie, and something else with hazelnuts—whatever you think would work."

"Since these are custom items and I don't have my own recipes, I'll have to charge you extra for their development. I'll need to make some trial pies."

"Sure."

"What's your budget?"

"Whatever it needs to be."

Right. I suppose for guys like Josh, the cost of the party will be just a drop in the bucket.

"You can take the list," I say. "Email me what you want, and I'll give you the cost."

"I also want to try every single thing that will be served."

"I assure you, everything will be top quality. You've already tried a number of our pies, haven't you? I can arrange for you to try the hazelnut ones I make specially for your event, but it's not necessary for you to—"

"Yes, it is. It has to be perfect. I want many different pies at this party, and I want to have tried every single one."

"You're a control freak," I say, before I can think better of it.

He chuckles. "Sometimes."

He leans forward, as though he's about to tell me something secret, intimate. He's got such a charming smile, and *God.* Usually I'm pretty good at focusing on work, but I admit, he makes it difficult.

Really difficult.

I inhale sharply, preparing myself for whatever he's going to say.

And then he steps back, much to the disappointment of my body, and taps the list. "I'll take this and get in touch soon."

I grab a business card from the counter. "Here's my email. And phone number." To my annoyance, I sound desperate, and then, to my great horror, something else pops out of my mouth without my thinking about it first. "I'm sorry about Wednesday."

He frowns.

"You know, the butter tart filling? On your lip? When I invaded your personal space?"

Sarah, stop talking!

"Ah." He nods, and the corner of his mouth curls up. "I didn't mind."

Heat coils deep inside me at his words. I can't help it.

He winks at me before putting on his jacket and heading out, but even as cold air blows in through the door before it shuts, my cheeks feel like they're on fire.

He was flirting with me, wasn't he? I might have spent most of the past dozen years in a kitchen, but I'm pretty sure I can recognize flirting.

Not that it matters. Some people are just flirty, and it's only natural that he would be one of them, considering how attractive he is.

Plus, nothing can happen anyway. I need to focus on my business, and for the next month—Pi Day isn't very far away—making him happy is my number one priority.

In a *business* sense, of course.

~

I get home at five o'clock—an early day. I'm not ready for dinner, but I help myself to a glass of the wine I opened yesterday. It's not like anyone else is here to drink it.

After checking Happy As Pie's social media accounts, I can't help myself from Googling Josh Yu. I discover his company has made a few of the apps I have on my phone, and I find a brief interview with him in a "20 Young Canadian Entrepreneurs to Watch" article.

This guy is some kind of tech hotshot. I can't believe I'm planning a party for him.

To my surprise, I also recognize another person in the article: Caitlin Ng. As in, the Caitlin who came into Happy As Pie the other day, asking for a pie buffet for her wedding. Apparently, she started the dating app Match Me. Huh. I wonder if that's how she met her fiancé.

I make my way through the search results and come across another recent article: "35 Most Eligible Bachelors Under 35 in Toronto."

So he's single!

I shut down that line of thinking. I did not move to Toronto to score a guy on some most-eligible-bachelors list. I'm here for the food and opportunities.

In the photo—because there has to be a photo for a list like this—he's got his arms casually crossed over his chest, and he's looking away from the camera, smiling. He is, once again, wearing a Henley. Perhaps it's the only kind of shirt he owns. Not that I'm complaining. He wears it well, and maybe no one expects you to wear a suit when you work in tech?

I picture him in a suit, his tie loosened, the top buttons of his shirt undone...

Okay, Sarah. Not a good use of your time. Think about Nutella pies instead.

~

Whenever I need a break from work, I take a short walk around the neighborhood. Saturday afternoon, after being in the kitchen for seven hours straight, I put on my winter coat and head outside.

It's not a nice day. The wind is brisk, and it's far below freezing. It won't be a long walk, maybe ten minutes, and then I'll head back.

I glance at the empty storefront across the street from Happy As Pie. It's been leased, and a little work has been going on there over the past month, but I've never seen anyone inside.

Until now.

I walk across the street to take a closer look. There are two women painting the back wall a vibrant pink. From the look of things, they're going to be selling some kind of food, and I'm curious to know the details. When I first opened Happy As Pie, there was a sushi restaurant here, but it closed down a few months ago.

One of the women—a petite Asian woman—glances toward the door and sees me staring.

Shit.

I turn to walk away, but she opens the door before I can leave.

"Can I help you?" She sounds guarded, suspicious.

"I'm Sarah," I stammer. "I own Happy As Pie. Just wanted to know what's going in here, that's all."

She nods and relaxes a bit. "A homemade ice cream shop."

An ice cream shop! How fun!

The other woman bounds to the door. She has dark brown hair and a wide smile. "You own the pie place?"

"Yep."

She extends her hand. "I'm Chloe, and in two months—I hope we'll be open in two months—I'll be running Ginger Scoops. Asian-inspired ice cream flavors. Taro, Vietnamese coffee, green tea, and lots of other things."

Is she Asian? I think maybe she's biracial, but I'm not sure.

"Cool," I say.

"This is Valerie, my employee." She laughs as she gestures to the other woman.

Valerie rolls her eyes. "I can't believe I'm working for you."

I get the feeling they've been friends for ages, and I'm hit with a bolt of jealousy. I imagine setting up my business with a close friend. Having someone I care about there for every triumph and setback.

In fact, I'm jealous of anyone who has a close friend, period.

"What do you think of the pink?" Chloe gestures at the wall. "Valerie thinks it's a bit much."

"Depending on what kind of look you're going for, it could work."

"I still think you should have gone with black," Valerie says. "Then you could have written 'Ginger Scoops' on the wall in blood red."

"Don't mind Valerie," Chloe says. "She's actually a very sweet person."

Valerie chuckles. "Thank you. You're hilarious."

"I should be going," I say. "It was nice to meet you both."

"Nice to meet you, too." Chloe waves at me.

I head down Baldwin Street, and when I'm back in my kitchen ten minutes later, working on some apple pie filling, I still feel a twinge of longing.

Maybe I should have asked, "Will you be my friend?" like we were six-year-olds on the playground.

[5]
SARAH

ANN POKES her head into the kitchen the next day. "There are some girls here to see you."

"Girls?" I say, wiping my hands on my apron.

"Well, they look like they're about twenty-five. They're girls to me."

I head to the front. Chloe and Valerie are standing by the counter, each holding a plate with a meat pie.

"It smells delicious," Chloe says. "I got the beef and mushroom."

"I have the pulled pork," Valerie says.

"We thought we'd stop in and see you for lunch." Chloe tilts her head. "Unless you're busy?"

"No, no. I've already eaten, but I could use a coffee break." I pour myself a cup of coffee and join them at a table. I feel like I'm auditioning for a role.

Valerie looks around. "Do you do catering?"

"We haven't catered any events yet, but I have our first customer lined up. The CEO of a tech company wants to throw a Pi Day party. He came in yesterday."

"A Pi Day party?" Chloe laughs.

"Which company?" Valerie asks.

"Hazelnut Tech."

"Ah." Valerie nods. "Yeah, I know them. They do mobile app and custom software development."

"Valerie used to work in that field," Chloe explains.

Valerie looks away, a shadow passing over her face. I want to ask her what happened, but that's not the kind of relationship we have.

Not yet, anyway.

She pastes a smile on her face. "You said the CEO came in to talk to you? Party planning doesn't seem like the sort of thing a CEO would normally do—he'd have some unlucky subordinate do it for him. What did you think of Josh Yu?"

"You really know a lot about this company," Chloe says.

Valerie shrugs, then digs into her steaming pie.

My face heats as I think of Josh, of the way he winked at me before he left yesterday. And the way he filled out his shirt.

And how he scrambled my senses.

"Based on your expression," Chloe says, "I'm guessing Josh Yu isn't a middle-aged man with a horrible comb over."

"No, he's quite attractive." Valerie takes out her phone and pulls up his picture on the Hazelnut Tech website.

"Ooh," Chloe breathes. "Very nice."

"I touched his lips," I blurt out.

God, what's wrong with me? It's like my mouth isn't connected to my brain.

"You mean you kissed him?" Valerie asks.

"No, the first time he came in, he got butter tart filling on his lip and I…" I shake my head. "I wiped it off! I couldn't help myself! Then I apologized for it the second time he was here."

I swear, I'm not normally socially incompetent, but I sure feel that way now. These women came here for lunch, and they wanted to see *me*. This is the best opportunity I've had to make friends in ages, and I'm screwing it up. I sound like a loon.

"Let me get this straight," Chloe says. "After you touched his mouth, he came back a second time and asked you to cater his party?"

"Um, yes. Something like that."

Chloe and Valerie look at each other, and then Chloe turns to me and grins.

"He liiiikes you," she says.

I feel a twinge of excitement at the thought but quickly tamp it down. "I don't think so. He's just flirty. He, uh, winked at me when I apologized and said he didn't mind."

"I bet he's interested," Valerie says.

"It doesn't matter. He's a customer and I have to be professional. This is my chance to start catering."

I don't quite launch into a detailed description of my five-year business plan, but I do tell them a little about my plans for catering and selling pies in grocery stores. It's been a long time since I've had people I can really talk to.

"We also do special orders," I say. "If you have to bring a pie to Christmas dinner but don't bake. Or if you want to propose to your girlfriend using pumpkin pie or butter tarts."

"Seriously? Those both happened?"

"On Valentine's Day. The butter tart guy wanted fifteen butter tarts, one letter on top of each tart to spell 'Will you marry me?' Then he contacted me the day of, wondering if he should have six more butter tarts to add 'please' to the question."

"So polite and Canadian," Chloe says.

"I know, right? I told him it was too late to make the extra butter tarts. I heard from him yesterday, though. She said yes."

For some reason, I picture Josh Yu proposing to me with butter tarts, and Chloe and Valerie being bridesmaids at my wedding.

What the hell is wrong with me? I just met these people.

Yeah, I really am starved for meaningful relationships.

Interesting that I was thinking about my wedding, though. Marriage isn't part of my five-year plan.

I talk with Chloe and Valerie for another ten minutes before they head back across the street to finish painting, and then I return to the kitchen, whistling as I work on the filling for some chicken and leek pies.

～

Every Sunday night, I treat myself to a dinner out.

I've lived in Toronto for over a decade, but I'm still amazed by all the food you can find in the city. After growing up in a small town with only a Tim Hortons and a diner, it's a luxury.

The cold spell isn't over, and a bowl of ramen sounds perfect. So I head to a place on Queen Street, sit at the counter, and order their special for the day. The broth is delicious, and the first spoonful makes me sigh in bliss. It's also nice to eat something I didn't cook myself. I love cooking, but I love eating other people's cooking, too.

I considered asking Chloe and Valerie to come with me, but I feared they would see the desperation for companionship rolling off me. Maybe next Sunday.

Sunday nights are my going-out nights because we close an hour earlier, and we're not open on Mondays. Tomorrow I'll make food that isn't pie, go grocery shopping, and watch a lot of Netflix—my usual Monday routine.

When I get home from the ramen restaurant, I settle onto the couch and call my mother.

"Sarah!"

I pull the phone away from my ear. "Can you keep your voice down?"

We go through this every Sunday. My mom talks too loud, I tell her to quiet down, and she does…for about thirty seconds, before she starts yelling again.

I asked Megan, my sister, if she had the same problem, and she had no idea what I was talking about. Apparently, Mom doesn't yell on the phone with *her*.

My bizarre theory is that she thinks she has to talk loudly to be heard in Toronto, like the entire city is one big cesspool of noise, and even in my own home, I can barely have a phone conversation. She was disturbed when I told her that I can hear street noise from my apartment (it's really not that loud!) and she's horrified by the amount I'm paying in rent for a small apartment.

Yes, my mother is one of those people who has lived in a small town her entire life and is scared of the city, and her mind is blown by the simplest of things. She rarely visits me in Toronto— she can't stand the traffic driving into the city, and I totally understand—but she's come once since I opened Happy As Pie. When I took her to Baldwin Street, she snapped a picture of the street sign, amazed it had Chinese characters on it. She wanted to carefully examine each restaurant, and she didn't understand how there could be four restaurants in a row. She wondered how they all survived.

Baldwin Village, despite its small size, has food from all over the world. Japanese, El Salvadoran, Indonesian, even a Korean-Polish fusion place. My mother and I ended up at the Chinese seafood restaurant. Although she's mainly a meat-and-potatoes cook at home, she's a good sport at trying other things. She enjoyed the food, though she was a bit weirded out by the tanks of lobsters and crabs.

"How's business?" she asks, her voice now at a normal volume. Temporarily, I know.

"It's not bad." I consider telling her about my foray into catering, but I'm not in the mood. "We had a number of special orders for Valentine's."

My mother taught me how to cook and bake. It started with shortbread cookies at Christmas—I would "help" with the cookie cutters and decorating from the time I was three. She taught me how to make pie crust when I was seven or eight.

Yet despite our shared love of baking, there's a gulf between us now. She didn't approve of my plan to move to Toronto. She wanted me to go to college in London, Ontario, which is about half an hour from Ingleford. London is a decent-sized city, but it's Toronto, the big metropolis, that I've loved since my first visit when I was seven.

I hear her words in my head again, as I do every time we talk. *You'll never make it.*

I'm going to prove her wrong.

We don't talk much about my business, soon moving on to her grandchildren—my nieces and nephews—and then my love life, one of her favorite topics.

"I heard about something new called Tinder," she says.

"I'm pretty sure it's been around for at least five years. And I'm shutting down this conversation right now. I refuse to talk about Tinder with you."

"Why not? Or...what's it called. OkFish? Such a weird name for a dating site."

"I'm not sure whether you're talking about OkCupid or PlentyOfFish."

"Ah. That makes more sense. Plenty of fish in the sea, yes. Toronto is a big city. Surely there must be someone in Toronto for you."

She's shouting again, now that she's reminded herself that I'm in the big city and everything must be at a high volume here. I don't bother telling her to be quiet.

"There's more to life than getting married and having a family," I say instead, despite the fact that we've had this conversation a million times before. "I don't need to be on OkCupid or Plenty-OfFish or Match Me."

"Life has no meaning if you have no one to share it with."

"No meaning at all? Really, Mom?"

There's nothing wrong with not being in a relationship, though I admit it would be nice to come home to someone at the end of the day.

I push that thought aside. A man would be a distraction more than anything.

But I will nurture a friendship with the women who work across the street, because that's definitely something I could use.

Fortunately, my mother changes the topic. "Your aunt Gabby showed me an article the other day, saying I just wouldn't believe it. I thought of you when I saw it, because you make pumpkin pie for your shop. Apparently canned pumpkin isn't actually pumpkin but squash…"

I let my mom prattle on about the weird articles Aunt Gabby has forwarded her in the past week, and she makes me promise that yes, I'll watch the video with the dog and the lemon, as well as the video with the dog and the sprinkler.

I end the call and sigh. Talking to my mother always takes a bit out of me.

I try to think of something pleasant.

Hmm… I wonder when Josh Yu will email me?

I can't help it. The thought of seeing an email from him in my inbox makes me grin.

I don't remember the last time I was so excited at the thought of a simple email.

SUNDAY EVENING, I'm in my home office, struggling to compose an email to Sarah Winters. This shouldn't be so hard, yet my latest attempt is a pile of crap.

I am most intrigued by the idea of the caramel pear pie. How much does it differ from the pear ginger crumble pie I had the other day? That pie was the most scrumptious thing I've ever had the delight of putting in my mouth.

Intrigued? Scrumptious? I sound like a pretentious ass, and "putting in my mouth" makes me think of—

Never mind.

I try again, focusing on the important information.

I am interested in moving forward with the plans for my Pi Day party. I would like to try the following savory pies: chicken pot pie, vegetable pot pie, and tourtière...

I also tell her which dessert pies I'd like to try, and suggest a time for meeting up.

The email provides the required information, but I'm not happy with the result. What tone am I going for? It sounds a bit stilted and formal. I want something...more casual? Friendly? Flirty?

I run my hands over my face. God, what is wrong with me? I'm just hiring this woman to cater my party, but some foolish part of me wants more than that.

Whatever. I push that thought aside.

See, here's one of the things I'm great at: self-control.

I wasn't always this way. During my wild years—when I was fifteen and sixteen—I didn't exhibit anything remotely approaching self-control.

However.

That was before the mistake that brought my rebellion to a screeching halt. Before my father stopped talking to me. Before I gave up on relationships.

Self-control. I have it in spades.

I'm not saying I'm an uptight workaholic who has no idea how to have fun. Nor am I a work hard, party hard type. I think I generally come across as friendly and easygoing, and a little charming when I want to be. I know how to have fun; I'm just very careful about the kind of fun I have. At home, I enjoy videogames and movies. I go out for beers with Amrita and Eduardo every couple of weeks, and if I feel like something more, I'll call Neil and we'll hit a fancy club.

I haven't seen Neil in a few months, come to think of it.

Maybe that's the problem. Maybe that's why I'm thinking of Sarah as someone other than the woman who's going to cater the party that will finally convince Dad to come to Toronto.

Yes, that must be it. I haven't gotten laid in a while, and going out with Neil is usually the solution to that problem. Neil *is* a work hard, party hard kind of guy, and he knows the best places to meet women who aren't looking for anything serious.

Alright, I'll get in touch with Neil soon, but first, I have to fix this email.

You know what? No. It's fine. It's straightforward and will do what it needs to do.

I hit "send."

Awesome. I've finished everything I needed to get done today. Now I'll—

Oh, shit.

I have a sneaking suspicion...

I open up the email I just sent, and my suspicion is confirmed: I did not delete the caramel pear pie paragraph. It appears below my name.

I cannot believe I made such a stupid mistake. I am not the kind of guy who makes mistakes like this; that's how I've gotten where I am in life.

But Sarah does something to me and...*dammit*. She's going to read those utterly inane lines and wonder what kind of drugs I'm doing. That paragraph makes me sound like a pretentious prick who's high on...I don't know what. I stopped doing drugs—other than alcohol and caffeine—when I was sixteen.

No, this definitely isn't just happening because I haven't gotten laid in a few months.

Sarah makes me feel things I'm not used to feeling. There's a desire that goes beyond a night in bed together. A kind of desire I'm not used to feeling.

I try not to think about that.

I grab myself a bottle of beer and turn on the hockey game, but my knee is bouncing up and down. I can't concentrate on the stupid game, not when I keep thinking of that email. I just hope she'll stop reading at "Regards, Josh" and won't notice the paragraph below.

However, the response I receive twenty minutes later reveals this is not the case.

From sarah@happyaspie.com: *I found your e-mail most intriguing, especially the postscript. I would be most delighted if you could come to Happy As Pie on Wednesday at 10 am, at which point I will have several scrumptious pies for you to put in your mouth.*

I bark out a laugh. I can't help it.

I'm looking forward to Wednesday morning, and I will try to

be on my best behavior. To be normal, rather than sound like a pretentious prick.

That shouldn't be too hard, right?

~

"I'll be back in an hour or two," I tell Clarissa as I'm putting on my winter jacket.

"No problem, boss," she says.

Amrita appears in front of me. "Where are you going? There's nothing in your schedule."

I might as well tell her. After all, I intend to send out an email later today with the details of the party, once Sarah and I agree on timing.

"I'm throwing a Pi Day party."

"You mean ordering a bunch of pizzas for lunch and buying some apple pies, like the math department used to do when we were in school?"

"No, I'm inviting everyone in the office—and their families— over to my house after work and hiring someone to cater the party. Which is why I'm going to a pie shop now to discuss the details and try some pie."

"Right. But why do you personally need to spend an hour on a Wednesday at a pie shop?" She looks at me suspiciously. "I bet the person you're meeting with is a very attractive woman, am I right?"

"Why would you say that?"

"No reason." She smirks.

Amrita is correct, but even if the owner of the pie shop were a foul-tempered man, I would be going myself. This party is for my father more than anyone, and I need it to be perfect.

I don't want to tell Amrita the true purpose of this party, however, even though she's my best friend and of course she'll attend. It feels weird.

"See you later," she says. "Have fun."

"Stop smirking!"

"I'll consider it."

When I arrive at Happy As Pie, the door is locked, so I knock. A minute later, Sarah ushers me inside. She's wearing a navy sweater and a white apron, and her hair is pulled back in a loose bun. My heart speeds up a little just at the sight of her.

"Hi, Josh. Ready to put some pie in your mouth?" she says, then covers her own mouth with her hand, as though she can't believe she actually said that out loud. Since she seems a touch embarrassed, my instinct is to put her at ease.

And admire the blush creeping up her cheeks.

"Mm. Very ready." I send her a smile that has worked quite well for me with women in the past, followed by a wink.

Sarah ushers me to a table filled with pie, and my mouth waters. God, that looks good.

"Alright," she says, all business now. "The savory pies are five inches in diameter, meant to serve one person, so there will be one per guest, and some extras. The sweet pies are nine inches—"

"Nine inches, huh?" I can't help myself.

She's blushing again, and I like it.

However, this is a business meeting.

It's hard to remember that when I'm staring at Sarah and all of those pies. She's so pretty. Her hair is light brown with gold highlights, and a few wisps have escaped her bun. I want to push them back behind her ears and cup her cheeks in my hand.

I fear I've gone too far. All I did was repeat the diameter of the pies; I didn't ask if she'd like to put nine inches in her mouth. But I can't pretend my mind was anywhere else.

Self-control, Josh.

She soldiers on. "I have the three savory pies you wish to try. I'll cut you a small piece of each. Best to do these ones first, as I heated them up for you—they should be eaten warm." She puts a quarter of each savory pie on my plate.

I try the tourtière first. It's meaty with a flaky crust, and I groan in satisfaction. The chicken pot pie is delicious, too. I've never had chicken pot pie before, so I don't know how it compares to anyone else's, but this has to be about as good as it gets. The vegetable pot pie is also pretty tasty.

"Good?" she asks. It might be a question, but her voice is confident.

She knows I'm satisfied.

Although Sarah blushed earlier, she's not going to blush when I compliment her food. She knows she's great at what she does for a living.

I like her confidence.

"They're amazing," I say.

I polish off the pie on my plate. I'm tempted to lick it to get the last of the creamy filling from the chicken and vegetable pot pies, but I restrain myself from using my tongue...

Which makes me think of other things I'd like to lick. Like her lips.

Focus.

Seriously, I'm usually the king of self-control and making things go the way I want them to, but there's something about her that makes me do stupid things like send that ridiculous email and get distracted by the thought of licking her lips.

It's damn inconvenient.

Sarah grabs an empty plate. "Now I'll cut a slice of the caramel pear pie you were so eager to put in your mouth. We'll see if you think it's as *scrumptious* as the pear ginger crumble pie."

I groan. "I really must apologize for that email. I didn't mean to send that postscript."

"You know there's something called the delete key? Or the backspace, if the delete key isn't working for you." She smirks.

Dammit, today has been a day of women smirking at me.

I put my head in my hands. "I know, I know."

"But even if you had managed to find the backspace key on

your keyboard, that wouldn't change the fact that you wrote the paragraph in the first place. Maybe you were reading some interesting literature, and somehow you ended up channeling the author's style in that email?"

I think frantically for an author's name. "Jane Austen. I was reading Jane Austen."

"Of course you were. That explains everything." She pauses. "I'm a little disappointed. I expected you to be more…suave. After all, you *are* number nineteen on the list of '35 Most Eligible Bachelors Under 35 in Toronto.'"

"You saw that list?"

"It might have popped up in my Google search."

"Ah, so you were Googling me." I lean closer. "Tell me what you wanted to know."

"Whether you really are a CEO. Whether your company is legit."

"You wouldn't have needed to read the eligible bachelor list to know that. And you did read it, didn't you?"

"I might have."

"Stop being coy," I murmur. "You read it. You wanted to know about me, and not just because I'm hiring you."

It's suddenly very, very important that she says "yes."

I wouldn't say I'm a man who always gets what I want. Exhibit A: my father still isn't talking to me. My business career hasn't been without its hiccups. There have been failures; there usually are many failures on the way to success.

And it's not like I can get every woman I want. I'm not Neil. Though I usually do pretty well with women; I'm not complaining.

But now, I really need this particular woman to admit to having a little interest in me, because I haven't had this strong of a reaction to anyone in ages. I have a good life, but I'd been in a bit of a funk for the past couple months. This woman and the party we're planning have started to get me out of my malaise.

"Yes," she says at last. "I did. I was curious."

"Mm-hmm." I rest my hands behind my head. Not gonna lie, it's partly so she'll have a chance to admire my arm muscles. I'm not above pulling a move like that.

When she licks her upper lip, I feel like I'm regaining a little control over this situation.

I have a taste of the caramel pear pie. It's good, but I still prefer the pear ginger crumble pie. Next, I try the coconut pie, berry crumble pie, lemon-lime tart, and lemon meringue. I'm getting full, but I'm certainly not going to turn any of this down. One, it's delicious, and two, I need to test everything so I can tell Sarah what I want for the party. They're all amazing, though the lemon-lime tart is particularly good. Even better than the lemon meringue pie—and I've always loved lemon meringue.

"So, what are you thinking?" she asks. "Do you want just a few different types of dessert pies for the party, or a wide variety?"

"The second. Now, what about the pies with Nutella and hazelnuts?"

"Still working on those. You can try them the next time we meet. Does next Tuesday work for you? Ten in the morning is good. A nice break in the middle of my work day."

"This is the *middle* of your work day?"

She shrugs. "It's supposed to be. I get here at six to start baking, and I try to leave before three, but often I end up staying until we close at seven. It's my business, and I'm a bit of a control freak at times."

"Yet you accused me of being a control freak last time."

She shrugs again. "I understand what it's like."

"Ten o'clock, next Tuesday. Sounds good." I should probably check my schedule first, but whatever, I'll make it work. Clarissa can rearrange some things for me if necessary.

"Now, uh." She tucks a loose strand of hair behind her ear, and once again, I'm hit with the urge to touch her hair, to caress her cheek. "It might be easier if you give me your cell number so we can correspond in the next week as needed. About the Nutella pie and plans for the party."

"Of course."

I give her my number, and she enters it into her phone.

"And also because you kind of suck at e-mail," she teases as she puts her phone away.

"Thank you for your insight into my e-mail skills."

"Always happy to help."

We discuss the timing of the party, then she walks me to the door and unlocks it. I'm hit with the desire to give her a kiss goodbye, but I muster up some self-control.

"Bye, Sarah."

And then I leave, before I lose my restraint.

"I finally figured out how to get Dad to come to Toronto," I tell my sister Nancy on the phone that night.

"You're getting *married*?" she shouts.

"What? Why would you say that?"

"Because it's the easiest way to get him to visit you in Toronto. He's not going to miss your wedding, despite the fact that he no longer speaks to you. I'm surprised you didn't figure it out sooner."

"I'm not getting married." But she has a point. My father would show up to my wedding.

Probably.

My idea, however, is much better.

"I'm throwing a big Pi Day party," I say.

She chuckles. "Yes, that might work. Who are you inviting to this party, Number Nineteen?"

I groan. "Nancy…"

Since that damn "Most Eligible Bachelors in Toronto" list came out a few months ago, my sisters have started calling me

"Number Nineteen". Whenever we're all together, it sends them both into a fit of laughter.

"Okay, okay," Nancy says. "Who are you inviting to the party, *Josh?*"

"It's a work party. I'm inviting everyone at Hazelnut Tech."

"And our parents."

"And our parents. You're welcome to come, too, but I assume you have to work."

"Dammit. Why is Ottawa so far from Toronto? Maybe Wendy will be able to go since Kingston is closer. You'll have to tell me all about it." She pauses. "I'm sorry. I wish Dad was more reasonable."

Yeah. If only.

If only Dad didn't hold seventeen-year grudges. If only I hadn't been so stupid.

Nancy and I talk about her kids and the weather for a bit, and then I end our conversation and call my parents.

The phone rings and rings. My father is usually the one who answers the phone in the house, but when he sees it's me calling, he'll tell my mother that it's "your son," and she'll sigh and pick up the phone.

Yes, my family is messed up, and I'm aware that the way my family operates makes no sense to most people, though I could say the same of many other families. Amrita's, for example, completely baffles me, just like mine baffles her.

I don't want it to be this way, though.

As it stands, I go to Ottawa once a year, for Christmas. Once a year, I return to my childhood home, loaded with presents for my nieces and nephews and sisters and mother. I used to buy presents for my father, too, but he threw them straight in the trash, so I don't bother anymore. I act friendly and warm, even though my stomach is churning, and I pretend not to notice Dad glaring at me. Occasionally, he makes snide comments, but not often; mostly, he just talks as though I'm not there.

Once a year, I put up with that crap for my mother and my sisters, and I try to see the rest of my family a couple other times a year at Wendy's house in Kingston.

I just want, so badly, for us to be a semi-normal family, but to him, what I did was such an embarrassment that it's unforgivable. Everyone else has moved on, but not him.

On the sixth ring, my mom answers. "Hi, Josh. Nice to hear from you. What's up?"

I take a deep breath. "I want you and Dad to come to Toronto for a Pi Day party."

[7]
SARAH

It's Thursday night, and I've been Googling Nutella pies, mousses, and other desserts for the past hour. I've blocked off some time tomorrow for experimenting in the kitchen, which is exciting. I don't get much time to experiment anymore.

I refined my repertoire of pies over the five years before I started Happy As Pie. Now we have our staples, and I can make pretty much anything on the list in my sleep. I've toyed with the idea of having a "special of the day" pie; perhaps when we start doing well enough for me to hire another employee, I'll do it. Maybe every day, or maybe just on weekends.

Anyway, it's fun to be creative. I thought about the possibilities when I jumped in the shower after getting home from work, and now I'm looking at recipes for inspiration.

The following morning, once everything we need for the day is made, and Fatima and Dylan are working on a big batch of beef and mushroom filling, I attempt two pies. Both have a chocolate cookie crumb crust, which should work well with Nutella. The first pie is a fairly simple no-bake pie (no-bake once the crust is done, that is), with a Nutella and mascarpone filling. The second is a two-layer mousse. The bottom layer is a sweeter mousse with Nutella, and the top layer is a lighter bittersweet chocolate.

I'm anxious as I wait for the pies to cool in the fridge. While I work on vegetable pot pies to put in the freezer, I imagine the look on Josh's face as he tries the Nutella pies. I imagine him tilting his head back in bliss, exposing the long column of his throat, his eyes closed...

God, I really want to make something he loves.

I doubt I'll get everything perfect today, but hopefully it'll only take one more trial to get them right. However, I won't wait until next Tuesday to tell Josh about them; I plan to text him with pictures once they're finished, and I'm practically giddy with excitement at the thought of him texting me back.

I know, I know. But I just can't help it.

Josh can be endearingly awkward one moment, then smoothly seductive the next. I suspect he turns on the seductive charm with many women, but the first...it feels like it's just for me. Like when he sent me that e-mail with the truly bizarre postscript.

It only seems fair, as he makes me feel a touch awkward, too. Like when I wiped the butter tart filling off his lip and apologized for it two days later.

We fluster each other.

Sure, I'm not a CEO like he is, but we're both competent, confident people in our regular lives, and we're used to being on top of things professionally. When we're together, though, it's different. It's new and thrilling.

I don't let myself think about what that means.

At two o'clock, I take both pies out of the fridge. I decorate the first one with chocolate shavings and the second with chopped hazelnuts. After I take a few pictures, I cut two small slices and call Fatima and Dylan over to taste them.

Fatima takes a bite of each and chews thoughtfully.

"Well?" I say impatiently. "What do you think?"

"My kids would *love* the first one," she says, "but I prefer the second, although the top layer isn't quite the right consistency."

Yes, I can see that now. Should be pretty easy to fix.

"Although I'd personally do something with banana. Nutella and banana is a great combination."

She's right. I'll ask Josh what he'd prefer and go from there.

"Strawberries and Nutella are pretty great, too," Dylan says before he tries each of my pies. "These are both really good, Sarah."

Ann barges into the kitchen. "Are you guys trying a new pie without me?" She grabs a fork and helps herself to a bite of pie from Dylan's plate.

"Hey!" he says. "That's my pie. Get your own."

I'm already cutting Ann a small slice of each.

"Mm," she says. "That's good." She tries the second pie. "Okay, that one's even better."

I try both pies, and they're good, but not perfect.

"I don't know why you aren't smiling," Ann says. "They're delicious. But I guess you want them absolutely perfect for that handsome CEO, don't you? You were flirting with him on Wednesday—"

"No, I wasn't!" I protest. "Not at all. What did you see?"

"Ha!" Ann points at me. "You're defensive. I knew it! Not that I saw anything. I just suspected it from the way you were mooning about the kitchen after your little meeting."

"I was not *mooning* about the kitchen."

"He's handsome?" Fatima asks. "I haven't seen him."

"Very handsome." Ann's smile is smug, as though she's particularly pleased that she got to meet him. "He's also on a list of the top thirty-five eligible bachelors under thirty-five." She takes out her phone and pulls up the list. Fatima and Dylan gather around.

"Ooh, he is very attractive," Fatima says.

"These lists of eligible bachelors are always full of straight men." Dylan shakes his head. "Where are the eligible bachelors for people like me?"

"Actually, this is a very inclusive list," I say. "There's an 'interested in' section, and four of the thirty-five men are interested in men."

"Oh, really?" He pauses. "Not Josh Yu, though?"

"No."

"Too bad."

"It wouldn't matter anyway," Ann says, "since he already has the hots for Sarah."

"Excuse me?" I say. "How would you know that?"

"Lucky guess." Ann smirks, and I can't help my cheeks from heating.

"Sarah," Fatima says, "you seem quite familiar with this list of eligible bachelors. Have you been studying it?"

Okay, this tease-the-boss business has gone on long enough.

"Thanks for all your opinions," I say, "but it's time to go back to work."

For me, that means figuring out how to make these Nutella pies the best they can be.

That evening, I settle on my couch with my phone, a large piece of Nutella Pie #2, and a glass of red wine.

I've been looking forward to this moment all day.

I pull up Josh's contact information, type out a text, then decide the message isn't quite right and try again. It takes three tries before I get annoyed with myself and just send what I have, plus a picture of each pie.

Nutella Pies, version 1.0. The first is mascarpone and Nutella. The second is a layer of Nutella mousse, followed by a layer of bittersweet chocolate mousse. Not quite perfect, but almost there. I'll have one for you to try next Tuesday. Which sounds better to you?

I wait. And wait.

Five minutes later, he still hasn't replied. I'm annoyed that he didn't reply immediately, but more than anything, I'm annoyed that I'm annoyed about this.

Josh could be at a fancy dinner meeting for work, having dinner with his family, or working out and building his lovely muscles. Or he could be in the shower, water sluicing over his skin and dark hair, down, down, down…

Get it together, Sarah.

To kill some time, I pull up that stupid eligible bachelors article and go down the rabbit hole of looking at the comment section. There are 1047 comments, which seems a tad much. Some assholes accuse the list makers of trying to be too politically correct by including so many men who are Asian and black, and a few who are gay. Others are thrilled with the list, and one of them compares Josh Yu to a warm loaf of bread slathered in butter…

My phone buzzes, and I drop it in surprise. I'd been so absorbed in the comments that I'd forgotten I was waiting for Josh to text me back.

They both look amazing, but I think I'd go for the second.

I stare at the text. It's a perfectly reasonable text, replying to the question I'd asked. Why do I feel disappointed?

I gulp my wine.

Yeah, okay. I admit it. I'd been hoping for something a little flirtatious.

I could also try something with Nutella and banana, I type. *Or Nutella and strawberries. What do you think? Would you find that ~scrumptious? Would you like to put that in your mouth?*

As soon as I send that text, I regret it. What the hell am I doing? He's a client, and I can't afford to screw this up.

Yet I have a feeling he will appreciate that comment.

Oh, God. Now I'm thinking about bananas, and how they look like…well, you know.

Fuck, it's been a long time since I had sex. That must be the problem.

I would like to put all of it in my mouth, he replies. *Both of those sound amazing, too. If you have a chance to try making them, go ahead.* He follows this up a minute later with: *Are you putting Nutella pie in your mouth right now?*

I take a picture of my slice of Nutella pie and my glass of wine, grinning as I do so.

Sarah, Sarah, he says. *That's not proof you're eating the pie. Just that you have a slice in front of you.*

Well, I say, *what would I be doing with a slice of Nutella pie other than eating it?*

It's a full piece of pie. Not a single bite missing.

This is true. I eat a bite, then send him another picture of the pie and the glass of wine.

That's still not proof, he says. *For all I know, someone else could be eating the pie.*

He wants me to send him a picture of myself? I hold a forkful of Nutella pie to my lips and take a selfie, feeling a little ridiculous.

He replies immediately: *Very pretty ;) You have a tiny bit of Nutella mousse on the corner of your lip. I would wipe it off with my finger if I was there.*

My breath catches, and then I do something truly ridiculous: I make a short video of myself licking off the errant bit of Nutella pie and send it to him.

Hot is his reply, and that single word sends a current of pleasure through me.

It's been a while since anyone has thought of me this way. It's rare for me to get attention from men, but to be fair, a lot of that is probably because I don't put myself out there. I don't have much of a social life, and I don't use dating websites.

And I've never had attention before from a man quite like

Josh Yu before, a successful man who looks like he could be a freaking swimwear model.

What are you doing now? I ask, so I can get the picture of him modeling swimwear out of my head.

I'm at the office.

Now I'm imagining him standing in front of a large window, looking out at the city below. Except instead of a suit, à la *Fifty Shades of Grey*, he's wearing a Speedo.

Okay, enough with the swimwear.

I imagine him wearing jeans and a Henley instead.

I need photographic evidence, I say.

Happy to oblige.

A moment later, I receive a picture of his face. He's quirking up one corner of his mouth and looking intently at the camera. It's not obvious he's at the office, but it's exactly what I wanted. Just a picture of him.

As I'm sure he knows.

This conversation is probably nothing to Josh. I bet he's had many such texting exchanges with women.

Yet I feel special.

I don't respond to the picture of his face; I can't think of what to say.

And then I receive another text.

May I kiss you the next time I see you?

My cheeks get warm at the thought, at the way he's asking permission.

Another text from Josh: *Just to be clear, you are free to say no, of course. It will not affect our business relationship. I will still have you cater the party.*

I appreciate him saying that, because mixing business and pleasure can get tricky.

I exhale unsteadily before typing my reply.

[8]
JOSH

I WANT.

I want to feel the slide of her lips against mine. I want to feel her melt against me. I want to taste Nutella pie on her lips.

I'm not used to feeling like I've lost my restraint. I'm not used to being distracted from my work.

When I'm doing business with someone, I normally keep things strictly professional. Friendly, but professional. I didn't plan for this to be any different, despite my attraction.

But I can't ignore it any longer. I had to ask if she'd be willing to take it further.

This isn't related to my business in the usual way. It's not like she's hired me to design an app. And when I see her, I get to eat pie.

It doesn't feel like business to me, but I'm aware that it's business to her. Her business is pies. This will probably be the biggest order she's ever had. The money isn't a big deal to me, but it's a big deal to her.

The level of anticipation I feel for our next meeting is, frankly, bordering on ridiculous. I don't understand this pull she has on me. She's a beautiful woman, yes, but there are many beautiful women. Why her?

Usually, I plan things out in advance. I figure out what I want, and then I figure out how to get it. It's all calculated.

But with her, all I know is that I want. I can't think beyond that.

I want to kiss her, I want to take her to bed.

And to my surprise, I also want to wake up in the morning with her, our limbs tangled, and hold her in my arms as we talk about everything and nothing.

I haven't seen her very many times, but I like how I feel when I'm talking to her. Relaxed. Like I can be myself. A little goofy, even. At the same time, though, I feel keyed up in her presence, bursting with desire. It's full of contradictions, somehow, but it feels right.

I guess that's the simple answer: I like how I feel when I'm with Sarah.

It's been two minutes since I asked if I could kiss her, and she hasn't replied. I fear I've read her wrong.

When my phone beeps, I pounce on it.

Goddammit. It's not Sarah but Neil, telling me about some "sweet party" he's planning to attend on Saturday and asking if I want to go.

The idea doesn't appeal to me, but maybe I'll feel differently tomorrow.

It's doubtful, though.

I could be in a room with a couple dozen hot women—if Neil is going to a party, this will certainly be the case—a number of them interested in me, and I'd be thinking about being in a pie shop on the other side of the city, eating pear ginger crumble pie and bantering with someone else. Leaning toward her, and hopefully...

Sarah finally replies.

Yes, she says, *you may.*

~

I'm going to a Nutella pie tasting. I should be thinking about Nutella pie and my party.

But all I'm thinking about is kissing Sarah. It's all I've been able to think about for days.

I knock on the door to Happy As Pie. The curtains are drawn, so I can't see inside. My heart beats rapidly as I hear someone unlock the lock.

Maybe I'll kiss her as soon as she opens the door.

Or should I wait?

I'm still debating when the door swings open, revealing two people who look nothing like Sarah: a young white man and a South Asian woman who looks a little older than me.

Good thing I didn't move in for a kiss right away.

"You must be Josh," says the man. "I'm Dylan."

"Nice to meet you," I say automatically, shaking his hand. Inside, however, all I can think is, *What the hell?*

"I'm Fatima," says the woman.

"We've heard so much about you," Dylan says.

"So much," Fatima agrees.

"Lovely things, I'm sure." I look around the shop. There are a number of pies laid out on a table, but Sarah is nowhere to be found.

A moment later, she walks out of the kitchen, looking sexier than it should be possible to look in jeans and a lemon-print apron.

I've really developed a thing for aprons.

"Alright, you two," she says. "Back to work."

Dylan and Fatima head to the kitchen.

"I'm sorry about that," Sarah says as we sit down at the table of pies. "They were, uh, curious."

"Why?" I lean toward her. "What did you tell them?"

She shakes her head. "Let's get down to business. I've got the strawberry-rhubarb, key lime, banana cream, and pumpkin pies, in addition to the Nutella pies for you to try. What would you like to start with?"

"Let's start with the pumpkin and banana cream."

She cuts me a sliver of each, and when she slides the plate over to me, I think, *Now.*

But I chicken out at the last second, which isn't like me at all.

Instead of kissing her, I try a bite of the pumpkin pie, and it's the best pumpkin pie I've ever tasted. The banana cream pie is delicious as well.

Sarah watches me as I eat, but she doesn't try anything herself.

No, that won't do.

I pick up a forkful of pumpkin pie and hold it to her mouth.

"I don't need to try my own pie," she says. "I know what it tastes like."

"Indulge me."

She parts her lips—God, her lips—and takes the bite of pumpkin pie from my fork.

I could feed this woman all day. I love watching her eat.

I have the impression she spends a lot of time at Happy As Pie and doesn't get out much. I'm suddenly overcome with the urge to take her to fancy restaurants so she can enjoy something other than her own baking.

She cuts a slice of key lime pie, and rather than pushing the plate toward me, she picks up a forkful of the pie—a bite with a little whipped cream and lime zest. She holds it up toward me and leans in.

I lean in, too. Even if she were about to feed me turnip cake or liver, I would be eager to taste it.

I slide the key lime pie off the fork with my teeth. Tangy citrus explodes in my mouth. God, it's good, and her face is so close to mine; I study her as I chew. She has a smattering of freckles on her cheeks and nose, which I never notice before, and her lips are full and pink, ready for my touch. Heat flares within me, and once I finish my pie, I cup the back of her head with my hand.

This. This is the moment.

"Sarah," I murmur, and close the remaining distance between us.

"Sarah!" shouts someone else.

The next thing I know, there's a stabbing pain in my upper arm.

[9]
SARAH

I CAN'T BELIEVE IT.

I just stabbed a CEO with a fork.

I'd fed Josh a bite of key lime pie with the offending utensil, and he leaned in, presumably to kiss me. But then someone shouted my name, jolting me out of my daze, and I startled, somehow stabbing Josh in the process.

Now, instead of kissing me, he's clutching his upper arm.

"Oh my God, are you okay?" I say.

Shit, shit, shit. This is something I've never had to deal with in the food business before. I'd never actually stabbed a customer until today.

I've screwed up everything. He isn't going to kiss me now.

I give my head a shake. That's not important. No, the important part is his business. He's not going to want to work with someone who goes around stabbing people with dessert forks.

I jump up to get a first aid kit. Fatima is standing in the doorway to the kitchen, her eyes wide. "Did you just stab him with a fork?"

"I did. Why did you scare me?"

"I wasn't all that loud. You were just off in your own world."

She clears her throat. "I'm sorry. I came out to tell you that the new mixer has arrived. You want to sign for it?"

I'd decided to buy a second thirty-quart mixer with the deposit Josh gave me—I've been meaning to get one for a while.

Now I'm afraid I'm going to have to refund that deposit.

"Thank you." I manage a smile for Fatima—this isn't her fault. As she says, I was off in my own world. How stupid of me.

But with Josh, I can't seem to help it.

I sign for the mixer, grab the first aid kit from the kitchen, and hurry back to the shop. Josh isn't at the table anymore, but there's light coming from under the washroom door.

I knock. "I'm so sorry. Can I come in? I have a first aid kit."

He opens the door for me then turns toward the mirror, examining the stain on his light gray Henley. I look closer. It appears the fork went through the fabric and drew blood.

"I'm so sorry," I repeat, stepping toward him. I roll up the sleeve of his shirt, except the sleeve is too snug around his arm, and I can't get as far as the stab wound.

The stab wound.

Jesus. This is such a mess.

"You should clean it." I open up the first aid kit. "Here are some bandages. I'll be just out there when you're finished."

"I thought you were going to play nurse?" He raises an eyebrow.

Is that supposed to be suggestive?

No, I must be imagining it. I just stabbed him with a fork, after all.

But here's the thing about the washroom in Happy As Pie. It's not huge, and Josh and I are rather close together. I find myself breathing heavily because of his nearness. Because I can't even roll up the sleeve of his shirt due to his big arm muscles.

It might be hard to believe, but I'm usually a pretty cool and composed person. There are minor disasters at Happy As Pie on a regular basis, and I handle them all as required, but right now, I'm flailing.

And then Josh takes off his shirt.

My eyes widen at the sight of all that lickable skin.

Focus, Sarah.

I have no idea what I'm supposed to be focusing on.

"Why did you take off your shirt?" I ask stupidly. I'm staring at his pecs, his arm, the hint of definition in his abs...

Oh, God. Am I drooling? I'd better not be drooling.

The corner of his mouth quirks up. "So you can tend to my stab wound."

"Right. Of course."

He leans over the sink. I help him rinse the wound—the four little pinpricks on his arm— with water, then clean it with mild soap. There isn't much blood. But still.

"I've never done anything like that before," I say.

"Stab a man who was about to kiss you, you mean?"

My breath rushes out. "Does it hurt?"

"Not much anymore, though it hurt quite a bit at the time." He pauses. "Perhaps I should assume you aren't interested in a kiss anymore? You're allowed to change your mind."

His voice is calm and collected, but he's breathing heavily, too. I look up from his arm to his reflection in the mirror. He's studying the wound, or maybe he's studying my fingers on his skin.

I apply a bandage. "No, I haven't changed my mind."

His hand caresses my jaw, and he tips my face upward.

"Tell me to kiss you," he whispers, "and I'll do it."

I can't get any words out of my mouth, but I nod vigorously.

He chuckles before dipping his head, and his lips brush mine. Once, twice...and then he's kissing me, really kissing me. His lips coax moans from me—and I rarely moan, not even when I'm eating my chocolate tart, which is my very favorite of all the things I make. I'm not accustomed to moaning when a man kisses me, or when a man grabs my ass and molds me against his body.

My body is aflutter with sensation. Everything he's doing is perfect. Utterly perfect.

I grasp his arms, which I've been dying to touch properly since I met him, and squeeze, and then it's his turn to groan.

"Sarah?" he says. "Maybe don't squeeze my right arm."

"Right. The stab wound."

"We can stop calling it a stab wound. It's really not a big deal." He removes my hand from his right arm and places it on his waist. I take the opportunity to scrape my fingernails over his abs and up his chest.

It's been such a long time since I touched a shirtless man. I hope I'm not making a further mess of it.

When he pulls back, however, I can tell from the look in his eyes that I haven't made a mess of it. It's clear he wants more, and I don't know what to do. I feel out of my depth.

Somehow, I manage to catch my breath and remember the reason for his visit today.

"There are four Nutella pies waiting to be tasted," I say.

"Just a moment," he murmurs. "It's payback time."

"You want to stab me?"

"I want to leave a mark on your skin."

I inhale sharply at his words, and my skin prickles with awareness.

He pulls aside the neckline of my T-shirt, then raises his head and looks me in the eye. When I nod, he sucks on the skin of my shoulder, and I can't help but clench my thighs. Can't help but think of him using his mouth elsewhere on my body. I arch into him as he continues to suck, then bites me lightly.

"There," he whispers, sounding pleased with his handiwork. He pulls on his shirt. "Now let's taste those pies."

How can he sound so calm right now? How can he sound like

he didn't just give me a hickey in the washroom at my place of work?

Dazed, I follow him out into the shop. I cut a small sliver of each of the Nutella pies and explain to him what they are. Although I want to feed him the pie myself, after the stabbing incident, I figure I should stay away from forks. Too dangerous.

He tries all the pies without saying anything.

"Well?" I'm impatient.

He doesn't reply but instead picks up a forkful of the Nutella and strawberry pie and feeds it to me. I close my eyes and savor it.

I really did a good job with that one, if I do say so myself.

"They're all good," he says, leaning close to me and sliding his hand up my leg. "I don't know how I'm supposed to choose, though I definitely want the banana one. My father will love it."

"Your father? I thought this was a work party."

"My parents will be there too, I hope."

Okay, my heart is like melted chocolate right now. He must be close to his parents if he's inviting them to a work function. His parents are probably really proud of him, unlike my mother, who is still baffled by my life choices.

I push that thought aside.

"You decide," he says. "Whatever ones you want to make, just as long as the Nutella-banana pie is one of them."

"You're the customer. You're supposed to decide."

"And I decide that I trust your judgment."

"Even though I stabbed you?"

"An aberration, I'm sure." He slides a hand up my thigh and presses a slow kiss to my lips. He tastes of Nutella, and it's glorious. After the kiss, he rubs the spot on my shoulder where he gave me a hickey.

I need to say something before I melt into the floor. "Would you like some individual-sized tarts at the party, too? I was thinking chocolate hazelnut and maple hazelnut."

"Sounds delicious."

"I'll make some for the next time we meet up."

"What about mini savory tarts for appetizers?" he asks. "Like mini quiches, and...I don't know what else. Or is that too much work?"

"Nope. You want to throw the ultimate Pi Day party, and I will deliver. Do you want to taste-test these ones, too?"

"If possible."

We discuss the logistics of the party and make a list of all the pies and quantities needed, subject to change once Josh has the final numbers. We also discuss having a few salads so there's something to eat other than pie.

Seeing the list of everything we need to make is a bit intimidating, but at the same time, I'm excited. I'm up for the challenge. We've already been making extra meat pies in preparation and putting them in the freezer. I'll have to make up a detailed schedule with everything that needs to be done and figure out how many extra hours I'll need from my staff.

Later. I'll do it later, when Josh isn't sitting next to me.

"I thought you might want to see my house," he says.

"You want me to come over?" I yelp, suddenly imagining his bedroom.

"So you can check out my kitchen space and figure out where to put everything on the day of the party. No other reason." He leans forward. "What do you have on your mind, Sarah?"

He knows.

He knows *exactly* what I'm thinking about.

"Why don't you come over for dinner?" he suggests. "You can bring those tarts for dessert, and I'll provide the main course. How does that sound?"

"It sounds amazing!" I exclaim.

I'm totally not playing this cool, but I can't remember the last time a man cooked for me. I mean, I'm not a relationship kind of woman and...

What exactly does Josh want?

I'm not sure.

But I want to go to his house, and if he wants to cook for me, I'll let him. I won't deny myself this. Yes, it's is a little complicated because he's hired me to do a job, but we can be adults about this and manage to do both, right? I trust him.

Maybe I shouldn't, because I haven't known him very long, but I do.

"Friday?" he says.

"Sure. Friday's good."

He drops a kiss on my cheek and walks to the door. Before he heads out into the cold, he winks at me—his winks are devastating, and he knows it.

I just sit there in a daze.

"Hi, Sarah."

Fortunately, when someone says my name this time, nobody gets hurt.

It's Chloe, standing just inside the door. "I saw Josh Yu leaving."

"I stabbed him with a fork and kissed him!" I blurt out.

My God, I'm going to scare off my new friend.

But she sits down across from me and helps herself to a slice of pie. "This is amazing. Nutella and strawberry?"

"Yeah."

She starts shoveling it into her mouth. "So tell me how you stabbed him with a fork."

I relate the whole embarrassing story, including the part where he took off his shirt and I "played nurse." She keeps laughing, but in a friendly way, not like she thinks I'm a total loser and can't believe anyone lets me out in public.

Finally, I tell her about our upcoming "date" on Friday.

"I haven't been on a date in ages," Chloe says, which surprises me. She's very pretty and good-natured, and she's probably never stabbed anyone with a fork. "Not with a man." She pauses. "Or a woman."

Ah. I feel I should acknowledge this in some way, let her know I'm totally fine with it, though I don't know what the best thing to say is.

"Cool." I smile at her. "I don't date because I'm too busy with my business. And you?"

"Well, there's that, and…" She shakes her head.

"That's okay. You don't have to tell me."

We're not telling each other everything, but that's fine.

We're still becoming friends.

I gather my courage. "What's your number? Maybe we could hang out sometime, outside of Happy As Pie. Perhaps Sunday night or Monday? Monday is my day off."

Chloe grins as she gives me her number, and I grin back.

I WISH I had a clean shirt at the office.

Alas, I do not, so I will have to stay in this gray shirt with the small tear and bloodstain for the rest of the day. With any luck, no one will notice.

I sit down at my desk, and I'm about to pull up my e-mail when Amrita walks into my office. Everyone knocks except Amrita. She always just barges in.

"I want to talk to you about the Langston project... What the hell happened to your arm?"

Ugh, I should have known nothing would get past Amrita.

"I got stabbed with a fork." I shrug. "No big deal."

"You got stabbed with a fork?"

Amrita's loud voice brings Clarissa and Eduardo, the VP of engineering, into my office.

Well, this is great. Just great.

"Amrita," I say, noticing something different about her. "Is that a new ring?"

"Holly thought I should have an engagement ring, too." She grins, then gives me a stern look. "Stop distracting me. What happened?"

"You know Sarah?"

"Who on earth is Sarah?"

It seems strange that my closest friend doesn't know about the woman who's been occupying an awful lot of my thoughts lately, but it's true, I haven't mentioned her to Amrita before.

"The woman I hired to cater the Pi Day party," I say.

"Nearly everyone has RSVP'd," Clarissa says. "I've been meaning to go over the numbers with you."

"Not yet," Amrita says. "I want to know what happened."

I sigh. "I was taste-testing pies, and someone scared her, and she accidently stabbed me with a fork. That's all. No big deal."

"Why was her fork near your arm in the first place?" Eduardo asks.

"I bet you were feeding each other pie," Amrita says. "Kind of romantic, Josh. You ask her out?"

I could refuse to answer and order everyone out of my office, but Amrita will bug me about this until she's satisfied.

"I asked her to come over on Friday," I say, "so she can see the party venue."

Amrita rolls her eyes. "Yeah, yeah. I'm sure that's the only reason."

"I invited her for dinner."

"You're cooking?" Eduardo asks, somewhat incredulously.

"I can cook," I say, folding my arms over my chest.

"Huh." Amrita puts her finger to her lips. "This really is sounding romantic. It isn't like you, Josh."

"Shut up."

"And sure, maybe you can cook a little, but can you cook for a woman who cooks and bakes for a living?"

I hadn't thought of that. It's true; it'll probably take a lot to impress Sarah.

And I do want to impress her.

I don't let myself think too much about what this all means. I want to spend more time with her; I want a reason to take my shirt off around her that isn't because of an injury.

And I want to take her to bed. I've been lying awake at night, thinking of how it would feel to move inside her, and I'm thrilled that I now know what it's like to kiss her.

But although I want her physically, it's more complicated than that.

Not that I'll admit that to Amrita.

"I'll figure it out," I say, my mind frantically trying to come up with something I could cook. Maybe I'll just have to order something.

No. That's the easy way out, and I don't take the easy way.

Amrita starts rolling up the sleeve of my shirt. "I want to see this injury."

"It's covered in a bandage. Nothing to see."

Like Sarah, she gets stuck just past my elbow.

I don't reveal my little secret: I was flexing my arm. Both then and now.

"How did you get the bandage on?" Amrita asks. "You took off your shirt? Or did *she* take off your shirt?"

"Alright. That's enough," I say. "Everyone out."

"Except me. I have to talk to you about the Langston project."

I sigh. "Fine. Except you."

Eduardo and Clarissa leave my office, closing the door behind them.

"So," Amrita says. "*Did* she take off your shirt?"

"No, I did. While she was in the washroom with me to, uh, tend to my wound."

Amrita giggles. Actually giggles, which isn't like her.

"Glad you find my life so amusing," I mutter.

"Fine, fine. We'll stop talking about your love life."

Interestingly, I don't flinch when she says "love life," even if falling in love is not something I ever intend to do again.

~

Later that afternoon, I meet my friend Melinda for coffee at a Starbucks.

I've known Melinda Leung for ages. We drifted apart in university, but after med school, she came to Toronto to do her residency. She hardly knew anyone in the city, and so we started hanging out again, the past far enough behind us that we could set it aside, even if it's still affecting my life.

She knows a lot of people in Toronto now, and she met a man and got engaged—I'm happy for her, truly—so we don't see each other as much anymore, but we still meet up from time to time.

We talk about our work, and then she says, "Did you see the video of the premier getting pied at Queen's Park?"

"Yeah, and for a split second, I was worried that you were the one behind it."

Melinda chuckles. "I promise that wasn't me. You know I wouldn't do something like that. Though I'm not going to lie, I kind of wish I had."

I look out the window and smile at the thought of the woman who made that pie. I tried her banana cream pie—and not because someone threw one in my face—and it was, indeed, quite good.

"Josh?" Melinda says. "What's up?"

"Oh, nothing."

I'm not going to tell my only ex-girlfriend about Sarah, not now.

COOKING IS HARD.

I don't cook a lot. I'm a pretty busy guy, and usually I eat out or order in, but I do know how to make fried rice and omelets and various other things. Nothing too fancy, however.

It's Wednesday night, and I've been in the kitchen for an hour. Sarah isn't coming until Friday, but I wanted to do a test run of everything, and boy, am I ever glad I did.

I have a fancy knife block with a wide selection of knives, not that I know what the difference is between them. Perhaps this was the problem. I randomly selected a knife to chop an onion, and as tears streamed down my face and my vision blurred—Jesus, those suckers are potent—I managed to cut my thumb instead of the onion.

It's a worse injury than the one Sarah inflicted on me, which has healed nicely.

I bandaged up my thumb and went back to work on the beef stew. I figured that would be appropriate for a cold winter's day. Nothing too fancy that screams, *I'm desperate to please you!!*

Still, I'm trying pretty damn hard here, without going

completely over the top and making foie gras terrine or some kind of fancy French sauce.

Now the stew is simmering, but there's a strange burning smell…

Shit! The toasted sunflower seeds! I was trying to toast sunflower seeds for a salad.

No sooner have I pulled the pan off the stove than the smoke detector goes off. I climb onto a chair and try to pull out the battery, but for some reason, the stupid battery won't come out of the smoke detector. Finally, I get it out, only to hear something bubbling over on the stove.

Crap. The stew. I take off the lid and turn down the heat.

Okay. I can do this. I run a fucking company; surely, I can make beef stew.

It's not like I thought cooking was easy-peasy, and I definitely had respect for what Sarah does in the kitchen. But now, I'm truly amazed that she's going to make—with help, but still—a hundred and twenty savory pies for my party, plus a large selection of dessert pies. How does she do it?

I've spent an hour in the kitchen and I'm already tired, but now the beef stew is cooking nicely, and all I have to do is wait another hour, then see how it tastes.

I sit down on a couch in the living room, which is right next to the kitchen, and open my laptop, determined to answer the e-mails I've been putting off all day.

The next thing I know, I'm jolted awake by the alarm on my phone, telling me the stew is ready.

Well, so much for my e-mails.

Also, falling asleep while you have something on the stove is really not smart, and I've already set off the smoke detector once.

Anyway, I'm rather hungry after my unplanned nap. I hurry to the kitchen, where I turn off the element and lift up the lid, expecting a delicious aroma to hit my nose.

Instead, it smells rather burnt.

Hmph. Well, maybe it'll taste better than it smells. I try a spoonful.

Nope, it tastes bad, too.

I order a pepperoni pizza and hope I'll do better tomorrow.

∼

Beef Stew Attempt #2 is a definite improvement over Beef Stew Attempt #1. This time, I don't burn it, and I don't cut myself while chopping the onion. It still makes me cry, but I can handle a few tears. The vegetables are too soft, however, so I won't cook them as long tomorrow when Sarah comes over. I write down a few other small changes to make, then help myself to a big bowl of stew for my dinner.

I'm not used to having a home-cooked meal like this. It's nice, aside from the fact that I'm all alone.

But tomorrow, I'll have company, and in addition to the beef stew, there will be salad with sunflower seeds that are *not* burnt, as well as red wine and bread.

I hope it goes well. I desperately want it to go well.

∼

"It smells delicious," Sarah says when she steps into my house. "What are you making?"

"Oh, just a little something I whipped up," I say, all cool, as though I haven't spent the past three days trying to perfect it. As though I didn't spend half an hour at the LCBO, debating which wine to get. As though I didn't spend another half hour trying to figure out the best place in the city to get a good baguette, then drove out of the way to buy it.

This woman. She makes me do crazy things.

She's wearing a purple sweater that's a bit lower cut than what she usually wears. It provides a tantalizing hint of cleavage.

I am mesmerized.

I hang up her jacket as she slips off her winter boots. We head to the kitchen, where she puts a container of tarts on the kitchen island, as well as a little package wrapped in red paper.

"I love your kitchen." She turns around and runs her hands over the granite countertop. "The one in my apartment leaves a lot to be desired. You have so much counter space, which will be good for the party."

"Glass of wine?" I ask, trying to be the good host. Trying not to pay too much attention to the way her skin is pink and glowing after being out in the cold, and the fact that we're all alone in my house.

"Yes, please."

I pour us each a small glass, and she has a sip.

"It's very good," she says, then hands over the package in red paper. "A sorry-I-stabbed-you-in-the-arm present."

"You didn't need to," I murmur. "You being here now is enough of a present."

Is that lame? Or smooth?

And why have I completely lost the ability to tell the difference?

The package isn't heavy. I rip open the paper and smile when I see what's inside.

Paper napkins.

That's right, I'm smiling because a gorgeous woman got me napkins.

The first package of napkins is printed with the digits of pi: 3.141592653589793... The second simply has a large π in the middle. The third is a math joke. A familiar math joke, which I last saw on my father's Facebook profile.

"Be rational," says i.

"Get real," says π.

The napkins in the fourth package—yes, there are four packages—say "Happy Pi Day," and there's a cartoon slice of cherry pie beneath the words.

"These are incredible," I say. "Perfect for the party. Where did you find them?"

She shrugs. "You can find anything online."

True, but it never would have occurred to me to look for Pi Day napkins. I drop the packages onto the kitchen island, then lean over and kiss her on the lips.

"Josh," she says, her voice all breathy from the single press of my lips against hers. "What are we doing?"

"I don't know," I murmur.

And I don't care, because it feels so damn good.

I'm not sure what will happen tonight. I just know that I want to be here with her. I've been able to think of little else for the past few days.

Casually draping one arm over her waist, I have a sip of my wine and examine the napkins again.

"A classic math joke," I say, picking up the third package. "You see, the digits of pi never repeat because pi is an irrational number, and i is the square root of minus one so—"

"Josh." This time when she says my name, it doesn't sound breathy and sexy.

This time, she sounds annoyed.

"Why do you assume I don't understand the joke?" she asks. "Because I'm a woman?"

I hold up my hands. "No, no. Nothing like that."

"Women can do math, you know."

"I'm well aware of that."

"But what?" She puts her hands on her hips. "You think that because I make pie for a living, I know nothing about math? It was my best subject in school, and I took multiple math courses in grade twelve."

God, I've made such a hash of this. And it had been going so well.

Amrita would shoot me for this. I'm acting like the asshole I swore I'd never be.

A man in my position can get away with a lot. If a guy's the CEO of a tech company, people might say he's a genius and put up with bad behavior. Temper tantrums, general douchebaggery...you get the idea. A woman couldn't get away with it, not without being called lots of horrible names, but I suspect I could. But I've always sworn I would never be that guy.

And now I feel like *that guy*.

Why did I say such a stupid thing? Was I trying to show off?

Of course I don't assume women are generally bad at math, but maybe, subconsciously, that combined with her career...I don't know.

I run my hand through my hair. "You're right. I was being an idiot, and you were absolutely right to call me on it. There's no excuse. I will do better."

She looks pleasantly surprised by my apology, which is a further indictment of my gender.

The mood is ruined, however.

I take a step back. "You know what would be cool?" I say, needing to fill the silence. "Cookies in the shape of numbers, so we could have pi out to...I don't know how many digits. A hundred, maybe? I know you own a pie shop, not a cookie shop—"

"I can make shortbread cookies, no problem. I'll charge you for it, though."

"Of course." I pause. "You ready to eat?"

"So this is just a little something you whipped up?" Sarah asks after taking a bite of beef stew. She slathers a piece of baguette in butter and dips it in the stew, then moans in satisfaction.

Good God. She's so sexy when she eats.

After the incident earlier, I feel the need to tell her the truth about this. There's still a bit of tension between us, and I want to defuse it.

"No, actually," I say. "I'm not much of a cook, but I wanted to make something nice for you. I made my first attempt at beef stew on Wednesday, and I set off the fire alarm and burned the stew and sliced my thumb while cutting an onion." I hold up my bandaged thumb. "It was a worse injury than the stab wound."

She's laughing at me, and I like it. I laugh along with her—I can totally laugh at myself for this.

"Yesterday," I continue, "I made another attempt at the beef stew, and it turned out much better. I actually ate it that time. Then I made it for a third time today, and I think I've finally perfected the recipe."

"I can't believe you made three batches of beef stew for me."

"I can't believe it either." I smile stupidly at her.

This feels like new territory for both of us, and I'm glad I'm exploring it with her.

It's much different from how my interactions with women usually go. Not that I'm a douchebag to them—of course not. I'm kind, and charming, and very clear that I'm not looking for anything serious.

Something I haven't made clear with Sarah because, well...

I cooked beef stew for her *three times*, for fuck's sake, and I don't regret it. The pleasure of seeing her enjoy it is more than worth it.

"I considered baking the bread," I say, "but I thought that might be beyond my abilities."

She holds up her wineglass. "Did you harvest the grapes with your own bare hands and ferment them yourself?"

"I most certainly did. I traveled to Tuscany to pick the grapes. Seeing the rolling green hills and old villas was such a hardship."

"Mm. I can imagine." She butters some bread. "Have you ever been to Italy?"

"Rome and Venice, yes."

"Do you travel a lot?

"Not a lot, no. I'm busy with work. I don't take much time off."

She nods. "I know what that's like. Though in my case, there's the lack of money, too. I've taken very few vacations, even before I opened Happy As Pie, because I wanted to save everything I made so I could start my own business."

Suddenly, I want to take her to Tuscany, or to wherever she wants to go. We could sightsee and eat good food. Then at night, I'd strip off her clothes, suck on her breasts, and slip a hand between her legs...

She's looking at me with her pretty brown eyes. "What are you thinking about?"

"That's a dangerous question. Do you really want to know the answer?"

"Absolutely."

"I was thinking about sex."

"With me?"

"Of course with you." I lean forward and slide my hand up her thigh. "How could I not, when you're making those sounds?"

"What sounds?" She drops her spoon and looks around, as though the room could tell her what sounds she was making.

"The moans of pleasure when you eat my food." I stroke her knee, and she makes some similar sounds, but for an entirely different reason.

"You've certainly got the whole romantic home-cooked meal thing mastered."

"Except it took me three tries."

"Yes, and you actually told me that." She twists her mouth. "Was that a calculated move to be endearingly awkward? To prove you're not too much of a lady-killer?"

I snort into my wineglass. "A *lady-killer*? Hardly. I just didn't want to give you a false impression that I'm amazing in the kitchen."

"Are you amazing in other places?"

I waggle my eyebrows. "Want to find out?"

"Absolutely. I want to find out how amazing you are at making a snowman." She gestures to the window. "We've had a lot of snow lately."

"Sarah."

"Yes, Josh?" She grins, then has another bite of stew. "Maybe I'd prefer to find out how good you are at making pies."

"Nowhere near as good as you, I promise."

"What about reciting the digits of pi?"

"I know forty. Impressed?"

"Useless knowledge."

"True," I concede. "I memorized them for a Pi Day competition back in university, and they stuck in my head for some reason. I'm cool that way."

"Mm." She twists her lips to the side. "Back to the question you were really asking...I haven't decided yet. I'm not sure I'm ready."

"That's fine. You're always allowed to say no."

I won't say I'm not disappointed, but I won't pressure her at all.

She twirls her wineglass between her fingers. "It works really well on me. The combination of awkwardness and confidence, like when you smoothly took off your shirt so I could tend to your wound. You knew I would enjoy that, didn't you?"

"Mm-hmm. I was right, wasn't I?"

She ducks her head. "Very right. But the weird email—"

"God, please don't mention that e-mail. I promise, I only act like this with you. You make me lose my mind sometimes."

"That doesn't happen with most women?"

"No. I'm usually in control of the situation, but with you, it gets away from me."

"You make me feel that way, too," she confesses.

Hesitantly, she reaches across the table, and I take her hand in mine.

I have a vague memory of feeling this way once before. I was a boy with his first girlfriend, and I adored her. I totally lost track of time, lost track of myself, whenever we were together.

Which was part of my downfall.

So the way I feel scares me, but I was a boy then, not a man.

Sarah is wonderful, and even if I decide to be a complete nerd and recite those forty digits of pi right now, she'd probably still like me. After all, I made that utterly inane attempt to explain a math joke to her when she had no need of my help, and she's still here, eating the food I cooked, holding my hand.

The fact that she's still here makes me want to do everything perfectly from now on.

One thing's for sure: I will never underestimate her again.

"Ready for dessert?" I ask.

JOSH and I are sitting at adjacent sides of his large dining room table, a single plate with two small tarts between us. One maple hazelnut, one chocolate hazelnut. He insisted on "plating" the dessert, adding a scoop of fancy vanilla ice cream along with a sprig of mint and a sliced strawberry, which delighted me.

When we were eating the stew, we were sitting across from each other, but now we're closer, our knees touching, and his presence is making it hard for me to think. He smells good, like herbs and wine—like a kitchen, because he's been slaving away in there, making a meal for me.

This man, who probably has much better things to do with his time, learned how to make a great beef stew for *me*.

Dessert, however, is my contribution to the meal, and I know it's good.

I pick up a forkful of the chocolate hazelnut tart. Rather than putting it in my mouth, I hold it up to his lips. The last time we tried to feed each other, I managed to draw blood, but I'll make sure that doesn't happen again.

He takes the piece of chocolate hazelnut tart into his mouth, and I'm mesmerized by his lips. By his jaw. By every inch of his body, really.

I was *not* mesmerized by the way he tried to explain the napkins that *I* had bought for him. Not that there's anything wrong with not knowing about rational and imaginary numbers. It isn't something I have to think about in my daily life. But he went ahead and assumed I didn't know and wouldn't have bothered to look up the meaning of the gift I got him.

Of course, it wasn't the first time a guy assumed he had to explain something I already understood, but I feel like Josh actually learns from his mistakes—which is rarer than it should be—and he didn't defend himself for his assumption. He's not one of these pretentious assholes who assumes everything that comes out of his mouth is spun from gold, even though he's been quite successful in life.

So, I think we're okay.

He swallows the chocolate hazelnut tart. "It's delicious."

"Why, thank you."

He helps himself to another bite of chocolate hazelnut tart, along with some ice cream, before trying the maple hazelnut one.

"This one's good, too."

"Which do you like better?"

"Why are you asking me to make impossible decisions?"

"Just curious."

"If I had to pick, I'd go with the maple one."

He holds a forkful of maple hazelnut tart up to my mouth, and I eat my creation.

It's better when he's feeding it to me than when I was eating it alone at Happy As Pie. I stayed at work late yesterday, perfecting these tarts for him, and it was worth it.

And then I blurt out something that I hadn't meant to reveal. "We've never catered before. I've done catering jobs when I worked at other places, but never at Happy As Pie. I've never heated up over a hundred savory pies and provided thirty or so sweet pies, plus tarts and savory tartlets—"

"Sarah…"

"Aren't you worried I'll screw up?"

"I have every confidence in you," he says. "I think what you do is amazing. I can't imagine making the pie crust and the filling, and then baking it—I can't even imagine making one savory pie, and you do it all so easily."

"It's a lot of work. I work all the time."

"But you do it. You're great at what you do." He feeds me a piece of chocolate hazelnut tart. "You impress me."

His words and the way he's looking at me so intently…it sends tingles down my body.

It's different from how I'm used to people talking about my business. My mom never approved, and we don't talk about it much, nor do I talk about it with my dad. My sister and brothers occasionally ask questions, but nobody seems impressed with what I've built. And I don't have any close friends.

None of those people understand everything I put into Happy As Pie, but Josh does, and he believes in me.

I feel *seen*.

Still, a part of me wants to duck my head bashfully at the compliment, but I don't.

"Thank you," I say, looking him in the eye. "I want to get into catering. I was thinking we'd be good for company lunches. Eventually I want to open a second location with a larger kitchen and sell frozen savory pies to upscale grocery stores. But that's a little ways down the line. We haven't even been open a year yet."

"Sounds good. I'm sure you'll do a great job."

I smile at him. On one hand, it's a little strange talking about my ambitions and my successes with a literal CEO. But it's Josh, and I feel like I can talk to him.

As we feed each other hazelnut tarts, my entire body practically throbs with awareness. It's almost too much to be sitting here, so close together.

I don't know if I want to go to bed with him, though.

I mean, on one hand, I really, really do, but the thought scares me. It's been a while for me, and with Josh, I worry it'll be too much and I won't survive the intimacy. Like, it'll completely change who I am as a person.

Also, I hear my mother's voice in my head. She's not one of those no-sex-before-marriage types; she knows that's not realistic. But even as she educated us, it was still made clear to my sister and me that we should abstain unless we were in a serious relationship. Sex was not something to be taken lightly or casually.

According to my mother's rules, I should still be a virgin, since I've never had a serious relationship.

But I've never been good at doing what my mother wanted me to do. I moved to Toronto, after all.

Why do I hear her voice in my head now? Why?

There's one bite of maple hazelnut tart left. Josh lifts it up with his fingers, dips it in some melted ice cream, and holds it to my lips. I eat the dessert from his fingers and suck the melted ice cream off them afterward.

He hisses out a breath.

Even that is almost too much for me.

What could Josh and I have together? I don't want to let my imagination run wild after one home-cooked meal at his house. Although he's been so sweet to me and said things I've been longing to hear, there's only been one night that could possibly be called a date. Plus, a fumbling kiss in the washroom earlier this week.

"Do you want both the maple hazelnut tarts and the chocolate hazelnut tarts at the party?" I ask, pushing those thoughts aside.

"Yes." He seems to look past me. "I think my dad would like the chocolate hazelnut tarts better...but I'm not sure."

"That's the second time you've mentioned what your father would like. You said your parents are coming to the party?"

"I hope so. They live in Ottawa, where I grew up."

"That's a long way to come for a Pi Day party."

"But it's not just any Pi Day party. It's the *ultimate* Pi Day party, and my dad loves Pi Day. He's a retired math teacher." Josh's expression sobers, and he doesn't quite meet my eyes. "He's never been to Toronto to visit me, and I'm hoping this will finally convince him to come. He hasn't spoken to me in about seventeen years."

My eyes widen. "Seventeen years?"

"Yeah." He sighs. "In the first half of high school, I was a bit of a rebel. Skipping class, coming home way past my curfew, getting drunk at parties, smoking pot."

"Sounds like many teenagers."

"Perhaps, but it was unacceptable in my family. I also had a girlfriend. My parents weren't quite the no-dating-until-you-finish-med-school sort, but they weren't pleased with that, either."

I frown. "So your dad doesn't talk to you because you had a girlfriend and skipped class when you were in high school?"

He shakes his head. "When I was sixteen, near the end of grade ten, my father was already yelling at me every day, and then…something happened, which he's never forgiven me for. He stopped talking to me, even though we lived in the same house. I cleaned up my act and started doing really well in school, but it wasn't enough."

I don't know what Josh could have possibly done to warrant that. I want to ask, but if he'd wanted to tell me, he would have. He doesn't feel comfortable sharing everything with me now, and that's okay. I'm glad he trusts me enough to tell me as much as he has.

"Whatever you did, seventeen years seems a bit extreme."

"He was particularly pissed because my mom had cancer and

was having chemo, and he hated that I was doing anything to worry her."

"Your mom…" It sounds like she's alive, but…

"She's fine now." He smiles faintly, sadly.

"Does she talk to you?"

"Oh, yes. She was disappointed in me at the time, but we get along now and I talk to her once a week. Perhaps I should just stop caring about my dad, but I still want him to speak to me again. I miss having a father."

There's anguish in his voice, and my heart aches for him.

"If anything could get him to come to Toronto and acknowledge my existence," Josh says, "this would be it. If it doesn't work, maybe I'll try to finally let go. I don't know if I can, though. He's my father, after all."

"Are your parents still married? And do you have siblings?"

"Yes, they are, and I have two sisters."

"Do they still talk to your dad?"

He nods.

"Do they try to convince him to change his mind about you?"

"They did at one point, but now they've just accepted it. I know it's weird, I know you probably wonder why I talk to any of my family at all, but this is what I'm used to."

Josh is a huge success now, and he's a good guy. I can't imagine any father not being proud of him, regardless of what happened in the past.

And then I wonder…

"Hazelnut Tech," I say. "Is this the reason you were so determined to succeed? Because you wanted your father's approval?"

"It was partly that." He laughs wryly. "But there are lots of things my father would have more respect for than a company that develops apps. He hates smartphones and still has an old pay-as-you-go cellphone. He doesn't understand texting at all. But, to my surprise, he recently got a Facebook account, which he uses to post lame math jokes. Like the one on the napkins you bought me." He pauses. "What kind of snake is 3.14 meters long?"

"Um…" And then I get it. "A Pi-thon. God, that's bad."

"Those jokes are what gave me the idea for the Pi Day party."

"You said he likes Nutella and hazelnuts. You want those pies and tarts for him, but what about the name of your company? Is he the reason you named it Hazelnut Tech?"

Josh nods. "I know it's pathetic, wanting so badly for him to properly acknowledge me."

"It's understandable," I say. "It's not at all the same, but my mother didn't approve of my plan to move to Toronto and open my own bakery. She told me I'd fail, and I'll never forget that." I tense at the memory. "I keep hearing her words in my head, even though it's been more than ten years since she said them to me."

"Maybe she feels differently now."

"But I know she still wants me to move back to Ingleford, maybe be an accountant."

"Why an accountant?"

"Because I'm good at math, and I took an accounting class in high school and aced it. I didn't particularly like it, though. Math was one of those things I didn't mind because it was easy, but I had no interest in it."

"Once again, I'm sorry—"

"It's fine." I wave away his apology. "Really, it is."

"I always liked math," Josh says, "but I often pretended I hated it. I didn't want to just be that Asian kid who was good at math, plus, as I said, I was a rebel, and my dad was a math teacher. Now I have this company that's probably succeeded in part because I worked so hard to make him proud, but at the same time, it's a company that develops mobile apps, something he doesn't approve of, to piss him off. Not that I chose it just to piss him off. I have a degree in computer science, and I saw an area where there was a need. The timing was good."

"Did you start it all by yourself?"

"No, Amrita and I founded it. She's the CTO now—chief technology officer. That's what she wanted to be."

His co-founder is a woman. Hmm. I can't help but wonder…

Josh quirks up the corner of his mouth. "You're jealous."

"No!"

"You are." He grins. "You're jealous."

Since he's called me on it, I ask the question that's on my mind. "Has anything ever happened between the two of you?"

"No. She's a lesbian, and besides, she's engaged now."

That's a pretty solid no.

He stands up, and I can't help but giggle when he scoops me up in his arms and carries me to the couch in the next room. He sits down with me in his lap and winds his arms around me, looking like there's absolutely nowhere else on earth he'd rather be.

I can't remember anyone ever looking at me like this before.

He presses his lips to the base of my neck and slowly moves upward. My nipples tighten, and I release a sigh of appreciation. When he reaches my jaw, he kisses his way along it and then, finally, he moves to my mouth.

When our lips meet, it's an explosion of sensation, and my body is even more keyed up than it was before. Every nerve ending is painfully sensitive, and when he cups my breast—covered in my sweater—I gasp.

"Okay?" he asks, pulling his hand back.

"Yes."

But he still isn't touching me.

"Josh, put your damn hand back on my breast!"

He chuckles, and I can feel it between my thighs. I wrap my legs around him as he returns his attention to my breasts, toying with my nipples through my sweater.

I'm not satisfied, though. I need him to touch my skin. *Need.* It's suddenly the most necessary thing in the world. I'm about to put my hands on the bottom of my sweater to pull it off, but he beats me to it.

"May I?" he asks.

I nod eagerly.

Perhaps I shouldn't be so eager. I could have put my finger to my lips and acted all seductive.

Fuck it. I don't care. My sweater is now on the floor, and Josh is unclasping my bra.

Or trying to unclasp it.

"I swear I know what I'm doing," he says. "I just...you make me so..." He shakes his head helplessly before finally managing to unhook my bra and throw it on the ground.

Once that's out of the way, he begins feasting on my breasts. He pulls one nipple into his mouth and sucks as he rolls the other one between his fingers. I arch toward him, wanting more, more, more.

I saw his bare chest before, but I've never felt it against my own. I pull his shirt over his head, then press myself against him, groaning at the contact of his hard muscles against my breasts. How does it feel so amazing to simply be skin against skin with him?

"Sarah," he murmurs into my hair. "I have to tell you something. The reason you couldn't roll up the sleeve of my shirt the other day? It's because I was flexing my arm."

I laugh. "You sneak! You wanted to have to take off your shirt."

"Guilty as charged."

My lips are still curved in a slight smile as we kiss slowly, savoring each other.

He presses his thumb to the hickey he gave me. It's mostly faded, but still visible. I spent five minutes studying it in the mirror the other night, unusually pleased that he'd marked me in some way.

The things he does to me.

I ache between my legs, and when I press myself against him, I feel the hardness of his cock, which shouldn't shock me, but it does.

I'm not ready to go to bed with him.

It would be different if I could just think of Josh as a one-night stand, but I can't. Being with him seems more momentous than being with another guy. It makes me feel vulnerable.

I stand up, then notice the open curtains.

Shit.

"I flashed the neighborhood," I whisper, scandalized, as I collapse back on the couch.

"I'm sure the neighborhood enjoyed it."

I swat his arm, then realize I hit the exact place where I stabbed him with a fork the other day. The bandage has been removed, and the fork-tine marks are faint. It appears to have more or less healed, thank God, and Josh doesn't seem bothered.

"Want to go upstairs?" He looks at me with his dark, seductive eyes. I don't know what makes his eyes seductive, but damn.

I shake my head. "I'm not ready for…" I gesture helplessly.

He grins. "You're not ready for me to fuck you?"

Fuck, fuck, fuck.

That word. The way he said it so pleasantly, but also with that current of desire.

"No," I say. "I'm sorry if I gave you the wrong impression, but—"

He puts a finger to my lips, and his expression sobers. "You don't owe me anything. I've made that clear, haven't I? It's totally cool."

A memory flashes to mind, of a time back in college when I was at a party—a rarity for me—and making out with a guy on a couch, surrounded by people getting drunk on cheap beer. He suggested we take it back to his place. Having no interest in losing my virginity to a stranger while half-drunk, I turned him down, and he accused me of leading me on.

That's why I said sorry to Josh.

He's right, though. I don't owe him anything just because he cooked for me, just because we're sitting here shirtless on his couch.

I do want to go to bed with him. I want to feel his talented mouth move downward from my breasts, between my legs. I want to feel him part my folds and slide inside me.

I want him desperately, in fact.

But I'm grappling with these unfamiliar feelings, with being in a situation that I can't control as much as I'd usually like.

I just need a little more time.

"Can I take you out again?" he murmurs, kissing the underside of my jaw.

"You didn't take me out today."

"True, true. Next time, I want to take you out. Somewhere nice. That okay?"

I nod. "Perhaps Sunday?"

And then he does something no man has ever done for me before.

He helps me get dressed.

First, he puts my arms through the straps of my bra and fastens it at the back. Next, he adjusts my sweater so it's not inside out and pulls it over my head, slipping my arms through the sleeves.

Somehow, it's tender and romantic that he's helping me put *on* my clothes, and it makes me want to take my shirt *off* again.

This man scrambles my brain.

He gets the container I brought the tarts in and walks me to the door.

Did I mention he's still shirtless through all of this?

Yeah. Josh Yu is shirtless.

And he's utterly gorgeous.

I gesture in the general direction of his bare chest. "I don't know how I'm supposed to say goodbye to you when you're only half-dressed."

He gives me a half-smirk, then retrieves his shirt from the living room and pulls it over his head. His expression turns more serious as he puts his hands on my shoulders. "I had a good time tonight."

"Me, too."

"Want me to call you a cab or walk you to the subway?"

I shake my head. "It's only a two-minute walk."

"Text me when you get home."

He kisses me on the cheek and I walk outside, smiling despite the bitter cold.

HERE'S the thing about cold showers.

When you live in Canada and it's winter, a cold shower is the last thing you want, especially when you're the idiot who walked to the open door without a shirt on.

But it was worth it to see the look on Sarah's face.

Sarah, the reason I'm considering a cold shower.

She didn't want to have sex with me tonight, and that's fine. She enjoyed herself. I'm going to see her again. Those are the important things.

Nope, no cold shower. I'm going to jerk off in a hot shower instead. No point in pretending otherwise.

I turn the water up nice and hot, and I brace one forearm against the wall. I recall the way her lips felt on mine, the weight of her breasts in my hand, the softness of her skin against my chest.

I imagine things we didn't do. Like bending her over in the shower and…

Oh, fuck, that sure didn't take long.

I've only been out of the shower for a minute when my phone rings. I hurry to my bedroom and answer it.

"Josh!" says my mother.

"Hi, Mom."

"Did I catch you at a bad time?"

"No, why would you say that?"

"You sound a bit breathless. Like you were running. Or having sex."

"Mom!"

She laughs. My mother rarely makes comments like that—thank goodness—but she does it occasionally to piss me off.

I'm not laughing. It's like she could tell exactly what I was doing, and that's disturbing.

"The reason I called," she says, "is to tell you that your father and I will come down for the party."

I clench my fist in victory.

Finally. *Finally.*

My dad will see my house in Forest Hill. He'll see all my employees. He'll see the life I've built for myself.

And I hope he'll be a little proud. Enough so that he might actually say something innocuous to me like, "This Nutella banana pie is pretty good!" Or, "Where did you get these napkins?" Or, "Gee, son, I'm so sorry I didn't talk to you for seventeen years after you knocked up your girlfriend."

I shut my eyes at the memory.

Melinda and I were young and stupid. And unlucky.

There was no baby. Melinda had no interest in having one; she wanted to terminate the pregnancy as fast as possible.

Unfortunately, my parents found out she was pregnant, and it was the last straw for my father, who was already pissed at me because I slacked off and partied. "We did not come to this country so our only son could embarrass us like this!"

The situation was beyond my father's worst nightmare. It was something he couldn't have even conceived of. (Conceived... haha.) In his world, good kids did not have sex. Ever. Until they were thirty and their parents decided they wanted grandchildren.

Dad wanted to kick me out, but my mother begged him to reconsider. She was sick, and he wasn't going to say no.

He grudgingly allowed me to stay in the house, and I was determined to get on his good side. I stopped skipping classes. I stopped staying out past my curfew. I cooked on the days Mom had chemo. I joined the school's math team, even though that was seriously uncool. I got a tutoring job. I taught myself how to program in my spare time because I was bored. Melinda and I stopped seeing each other, though we remained friends.

Her parents were angry at the time, but they're proud of her now. She's a gynecologist and prominent sex-ed advocate who's sometimes interviewed on the news.

I wonder if my father would be proud of me if I went to med school.

It doesn't matter, though. I never wanted to be a doctor, and there are limits to how far I'll go to please my family.

But now my parents are actually coming to Toronto to visit me for the first time.

When I get off the phone with my mother, I text Sarah. She's become the first person I want to share news with, even though I haven't known her for long. Funny how that happened.

I told her the reason for the party. I told her a little about my family.

It's rare for me to do that.

I don't think about what this means.

For now, the knowledge that my parents are coming to my Pi Day party and I have a date with a pretty woman on Sunday makes me smile, and I don't want to think about anything else.

"Where should we go for lunch?" I ask Amrita. It's Saturday, but we had work to do this morning, so we're at the office.

She responds with a smirk.

Oh, crap. She probably wants to go to the ramen place I hate. Most people like it, but they always screw up my order, and the last time we went, there was a rather painful…incident.

"No," I say, shuddering at the memory, "we're not going to the ramen—"

"You're right. We're not." Amrita bounces on her toes. "We're having pie!"

I groan. I know exactly where this is going.

"The pie place that's catering your party," she says, "it's on Baldwin Street, right? It's above freezing today, so walking there shouldn't be too bad."

"Except the streets are covered in slush."

Amrita waves this away, her new engagement ring glinting in the rather harsh light of my office. "I want to meet Sarah, and I want to taste-test this pie. Make sure it's good enough for Hazelnut Tech's Pi Day party."

I scrub my hands over my face.

"That reminds me," she says. "I forgot to ask—how was your date yesterday?"

"Good."

"I can't wait to get Sarah's opinion of it."

"She enjoyed herself, don't you worry. No need to ask intrusive questions."

"Ooh, exactly how good was it?" She gives me an assessing look. "Hmm. You're a little grumpy today, so I'm guessing you didn't get laid. Am I right?"

Part of the reason I'm grumpy is that I stayed up late, trying to plan our date tomorrow. Sarah is a foodie; I can't just take her to any old restaurant. It has to have amazing food. There are hole-in-the-wall restaurants with amazing food, but I want to take her somewhere fancy, where she wouldn't normally go.

Anyway, I finally figured it out, and since it's a Sunday, it wasn't too hard to make a reservation.

"Josh?" Amrita says. "You're a bit spaced out."

"Sorry."

"You going to answer my question? Did you do it?"

I glare at her.

"That's a no," she says.

"Don't get me wrong. There was definitely some nudity."

"Interesting, interesting."

"We're not talking about this anymore, and we're not going to Happy As Pie for lunch. You can meet Sarah at the party."

"Don't you want tender lamb braised in red wine with rosemary and carrots, covered in a flaky, buttery crust? Mm. And pear ginger crumble pie sounds like exactly the sort of thing you would like. Sweet fruit and spices and a crumble topping that's very...crumbly. And sweet and crunchy? I'm not sure, but I bet it's delicious. Or perhaps you'd prefer lemon-lime tart, with just the perfect hint of sourness."

Dammit. Apparently she read the menu online, and now she's tempting me with descriptions of the food. She knows exactly what I like.

"Can we go?" she asks.

I groan. "Fine. We can go to Happy As Pie."

Half an hour later, we walk in the door to the pie shop, and the delicious aromas hit me immediately. My heart also starts thumping a little quickly at the thought of seeing Sarah. I feel a twinge of disappointment that she isn't behind the counter.

"Hi, Josh," says the woman who's served me before. I think her name is Ann. "What can I get for you today?"

"I'll have the braised lamb and rosemary pie, plus a slice of pear ginger crumble pie."

Amrita laughs. "I'll have the pulled pork pie and a butter tart." She cocks her head to the side. "Are you Sarah?"

Ann shakes her head. "I can get her for you."

"Ooh, yes. That would be wonderful."

"It's really not necessary," I say. "I don't have anything I need to discuss with her today."

"Ah, but it is necessary," Amrita says. "There was that thing... you know, the *thing* we were talking about."

"Of course," I mutter. "The *thing*. How could I forget?"

I'm conflicted. I can't help wanting to see Sarah, but I'm not keen on Amrita meeting her. Sarah and I have a pretty good thing going right now, and I'm afraid of what my best friend will say.

"I'll be right back," Ann says with a smile.

Amrita and I take a seat and wait for Sarah, plus our pies. There are a few other people by the window, but it's not too busy.

"Please behave," I say to Amrita.

She pretends to be offended. "When don't I behave?"

I raise an eyebrow, then start counting off on my fingers. "Second year. That party with—"

"Hi, Josh."

I look up. It's Sarah, and I can't help but smile.

"It's so nice to meet you," Amrita gushes. "I've heard so much about you. Josh talks about you all the time."

"Does he?" Sarah sounds slightly alarmed.

"Almost never, to be honest, which is why I decided I had to meet you."

Sarah tentatively sits down at the table, as though she's afraid there's a whoopee cushion on the seat.

"The other option for lunch," Amrita continues, "was a ramen restaurant, but Josh had an unfortunate accident the last time we were there."

Oh, no.

"An unfortunate accident." Sarah leans forward, a little too interested for my liking. "Do tell."

"No, don't tell," I say, though I know it's futile.

"Now I'm very intrigued."

"So, this is what happened," Amrita says. "On the way to our table, the waitress stumbled and tipped two bowls of ramen onto Josh's lap."

"Oh, crap," Sarah says, a hand coming up to her mouth.

"These were piping hot bowls. Like, the broth was really, really hot. And you know how men can be rather delicate in certain areas? Well. Josh spent all afternoon Googling 'dick burns' before going to the doctor."

Sarah bursts into laughter, then sobers. "Sorry. I'm sure it was really, uh, painful."

"It was only a minor burn," I say, "and I handled it like a champ."

"Yeah, sure you did," Amrita says. "You were whining all afternoon."

This won't do.

"Just to be clear." I turn to Sarah. "There's no lasting damage, and everything is in proper working order."

"Ah, so you haven't had sex yet." Amrita nods. "I was right."

"Amrita," I say.

She grins. "It's payback, you see." She holds up her ring. "I'm engaged, and the first time Josh met my fiancée-to-be, he spent all evening telling her embarrassing stories about me."

"This is true," I admit. "There were just so many stories. I couldn't hold them all in."

"So now I get to do the same thing to you!" she says brightly.

It's okay, I tell myself. Amrita isn't going to tell Sarah about Melinda, or anything like that. The penis-burn story is probably as bad as it'll get. Maybe she'll also tell a few stories from university. I was a pretty good kid in those days, studying hard and getting good grades to make my parents proud, but I still went out on Saturday nights. There's that keg-stand story...

"Anyway," Amrita continues, "this one time in third year, we were at a party, and some of the guys were doing keg stands..."

Yep, I knew it.

Our pies arrive, and Amrita finishes the story as she cuts open her steaming pie. God, I can't wait to eat this.

"So tell me about you," Amrita says to Sarah. "Are you from Toronto?"

"A small town near London called Ingleford."

"Were you desperate to escape?"

"Very."

"You won't go back to your hometown and settle down with your high school sweetheart or anything like that?"

"Oh, God, no."

Amrita laughs, then digs into her pie. "This really is delicious. Josh was right."

"What did he say?" Sarah asks.

"Oh, just that your food was as good as a blowjob."

I almost choke on my pie, and Sarah's cheeks turn pink. She's so pretty like that, but this awkward conversation needs to come to an end. Right now.

"I didn't say that," I protest.

"I also heard that you stabbed him with a fork," Amrita says.

Sarah's cheeks are now practically red. "That was an accident."

"I know. But even though I wasn't there, I'm going to tell that story at your wedding one day."

I jerk my head toward my friend. Still, I don't feel as horrified by the idea as I normally would, which is…interesting. I haven't even had a real relationship since Melinda, and I was only a teenager back then.

A few minutes later, when Amrita and I are halfway through our meat pies, Sarah gets up and says she has to get back to work. I give her a quick kiss on the cheek—if I kissed her on the lips, there's no way it would be quick—before she leaves.

"I approve," Amrita says.

"She hardly got to say anything because you kept telling embarrassing stories."

"Was that me? Sorry, sometimes I lose control of my mouth."

"Sometimes?" I try to glare at her, but I'm in a good mood,

because I just saw Sarah and we're going out tomorrow night, so I end up smiling instead.

Amrita shakes her head. "Man, I'm not used to seeing you like this."

Yeah, I'm not used to it, either.

And I'm not sufficiently in denial to think that once I sleep with Sarah a couple times, she'll be out of my system. Oh, no. I don't think that will be anywhere near enough. The more time I spend with her, the more I want her.

I was her in so many ways.

In my bed, against the door, in the shower.

I also want long walks together. Movies. Picnics. Trips to far-flung locations.

This is uncharted territory for me.

🐾 I HAVE a tiny office at Happy As Pie, where I go over bills and orders and business stuff. Sunday afternoon, I walk into the office, and something decidedly unrelated to my business is sitting on the desk.

A pile of used romance novels.

Two Weeks with the CEO. Around the World with the CEO. A Secret Baby for the CEO. Pregnant with the CEO's Twins. The CEO's Quintuplet Surprise.

I drop the last book in horror.

Five babies? That sounds like a freaking nightmare. Presumably the CEO is rich enough to afford lots of help, but imagine all the diapers!

Dear God.

"I see you found the books," Ann says from the doorway.

"Um, yes. Why did you get these for me?"

"Because you have a date with a CEO tonight, right?"

"Yes…"

"Inspiration!"

"I see."

"Don't tell me you're too much of a snob to read romance novels."

"No, no. I'm not much of a reader now, but I used to read my mom's Harlequins all the time when I was a teenager."

As I read her books, I'd dream of escaping to the city, having a glamorous life and sophisticated husband...and being the pastry chef at some exclusive restaurant.

My dreams changed somewhat over the years. I nixed the husband. I wanted the career, more than anything; I didn't have time to search for the perfect man to make a baby—or, God forbid, five identical babies—with me. I didn't have time for a fancy lifestyle, didn't have time to go jetting off to Rome with barely a day's notice. The food industry is hard work, but work I'm totally prepared to do.

I look at the stack of books. "Why am I going out with him? I don't have time for a relationship. I don't have time for distractions."

"Yes, you do. You work too hard. You'll burn out, Sarah."

At times, Ann, who's fifteen years older than me, is a motherly figure of sorts, even though I'm the boss.

I think of my own mother. *You'll never make it.*

I have to do this. The alternative is unthinkable. I can't go back to Ingleford. My high school sweetheart—if Daniel Spiers can even be called that—is unavailable; last I heard, he had a wife, a tractor shop, and a baby girl he'd named after a tractor. I can't remember which brand, but I remember thinking that at least she wasn't named Johndeere. And I have zero interest in him anyway, zero interest in living within walking distance of my parents.

I need to make sure Happy As Pie succeeds.

For one glorious moment, however, I imagine I can have it all. The man *and* the business. Not just any man, but one who's a goddamn CEO.

Though honestly, Josh seems like a "CEO-lite" compared to the ones I suspect I'll find within the pages of these books. His business isn't an international empire, and it's not like he has a private jet and an island in the Caribbean.

Though maybe he has a nice vacation property. Hmm.

And it's not like he exudes sophisticated taste with everything he does. I mean, the man wears Henleys to the office, not designer suits, though they do look pretty sexy on him.

What will he wear tonight? What should *I* wear tonight?

I'll worry about that later. Right now, I need to be in the kitchen.

"I'd better get back to work," I say to Ann. "That cherry pie filling won't make itself."

Chloe texts me at four, asking if I want to hang out tonight. I tell her I have a date with Josh, and she goes a little crazy with emojis. She also offers to come over and help me pick out an outfit. I figure I could use the help, so I invite her over after work.

I try on my nicest pair of black pants and a pink blouse, but she shakes her head when I come out of the bedroom.

"Do you have a dress?" she asks. "Not that you have to wear a dress if that's not your thing, but you'd look good in one. Something that would go with these." She holds up a pair of high black boots.

"I can't wear those!" I protest.

"But you own them!"

"Because they were on sale. I shouldn't have bought them. They've never been worn."

"I bet you'd look amazing."

I smile. I can't help myself. It's nice having someone else around, even if I don't agree with her. I remember getting ready for prom with my high school friends, girls I only talk to a few times a year now.

I have the sudden urge to hug Chloe, but that might weird her out.

"Let me look in your closet," she says.

"It's a mess."

"I'm sure it's better than mine."

Ten minutes later, I'm dressed in a black halter dress with a few sequins on the bodice, as well as the boots, and Chloe is fixing my hair.

"There," she says. "You look hot."

"Thank you." I catch a glimpse of myself in the mirror, and damn, I do look hot. "But I can't walk in these things."

She waves this away. "He's picking you up, right? I bet you'll hardly have to walk at all tonight, and it's not like he can't afford to get a taxi, or that he's not strong enough to carry you."

I remember him carrying me to his couch the other night.

Yeah, he's definitely strong.

"I feel guilty," I admit. "A night out with a guy...it seems frivolous."

"Sarah! It's one night. When was the last time you had a night out like this?"

"I, um, really have no idea."

"You deserve it."

I burst into laughter, but Chloe doesn't join me.

"Really," she says. "You deserve a night just for yourself, and then tomorrow, we can go out for lunch and you can tell me about it, okay? Twenty-four hours without thinking about your business. Come on, you can do it."

Chloe and Ann have a point. The only time I really had a break from work was the four days I shut down Happy As Pie for Christmas and went to Ingleford, but I still spent lots of time crunching numbers and thinking of changes I could make.

A woman deserves a real break every now and then, right?

I'm going to have a fun night out with Josh, and then we're

going to have sex. I wasn't ready last time, tempting as it was, but tonight, I'm ready.

I wanted to jump him when he came into the pie shop yesterday, but somehow I managed to restrain myself and listen to Amrita's stories about him. I was a bit jealous, but not in the way I was jealous of Amrita when I first heard about her.

I was jealous that Josh had a close friend.

Someday, I want to have a friend who can tell lots of embarrassing stories about me, because we know each other so well. Not stories from my childhood, but stories of my adult life.

I imagine Chloe saying, *"Remember that time Sarah went on a date with a CEO?"*

Alright. For the next twenty-four hours, I won't think about my business. I'll just enjoy myself. I don't know exactly where this night will take me, but I'm ready. I'm ready for something exciting and unfamiliar, with a man who makes me feel like no one else.

Josh is five minutes early. I'm still transferring everything from my everyday purse to my fancy purse when there's a knock on the door.

I open it and attempt a smile, but instead, my jaw hits the floor.

Josh is wearing a gray suit, no tie, and he's leaning against the door frame, hands in his pockets. He looks amazing. Like, even tastier than my chocolate tart.

"I want to eat you!" I blurt out.

Dear God, what is wrong with me? Why am I acting like an idiot?

Maybe this is just what happens when you don't go on a date for years. You get so out of practice that when an attractive man appears at your door, you start sounding like a cannibal. I feel like I just showed up in a pumpkin costume to a party where everyone is wearing ball gowns.

"I mean...I can't wait to eat dinner," I say hurriedly. "I'm starving."

Josh smirks. Unlike me, he's calm, cool, and collected.

He touches my bare shoulder and pulls me toward him. "I want to eat you, too."

When he says it, it doesn't sound stupid. It sounds seductive. How unfair.

"You look amazing, Sarah," he murmurs, and then he nibbles his way up my neck to my earlobe, which he gently bites. He picks up the jacket I left on the bench and helps me into it, one arm and then the other. It feels so intimate to have him helping me with this, something I could easily do myself.

He leads me downstairs, where there is a nice black car—I don't know anything about cars, but it looks nice—waiting. I soon discover that Josh is not actually driving this car himself; instead, there's a driver. Huh.

He helps me into the back seat and holds my hand throughout the entire ten-minute journey. We pull up in front of a bank tower in the financial district, and I'm momentarily confused. I don't see any restaurants, except for a generic bar—is that where he's taking me?

And then I remember.

There's a restaurant at the top of this building, on the fifty-second floor, called Loren's.

I've never been here before. It's expensive, and there's lots of wonderful food in Toronto that's comfortably within my budget, unlike this place.

I turn to Josh to protest, then zip my mouth shut. I might not be able to afford this, but he can, and I won't tell myself I don't deserve it.

Our table is by the window, and the view is amazing. I can see the CN Tower, the city all lit up before us.

"Is this okay?" Josh asks me, and he sounds uncertain, just a tiny bit.

That makes me melt.

"It's perfect." I smile at him. "I've always wanted to go here."

He tugs at the collar of his dress shirt. He doesn't seem comfortable dressed up like this, but he's doing it. For me.

"I haven't gone out on a date in three years," I blurt out, because I seem to lose control of my mouth around him.

"I haven't been on a date in a while, either," he admits.

I suppose Friday night was a date of sorts, but we didn't go out. He cooked for me. This is a little different.

In three days, Josh has cooked dinner for me and taken me to a fancy restaurant. He must really like me.

I look at him as he peruses the menu, and my heart flutters.

"What are you getting?" he asks.

Oops. I haven't even looked at the menu because I've just been staring at him.

"I'm not sure yet," I say.

I end up ordering burrata for my appetizer, which comes with beets and herbs and lavash, and elk with sour cherry reduction for my main course. Josh orders us a bottle of red wine, and it doesn't take long to come, followed by our appetizers. Josh has rabbit, but I'm sure it's nowhere near as good as my burrata.

I tear open the outer shell with my fork, and the creamy interior oozes out. I scoop some onto the lavash and bite into it, and oh my God, it's amazing. I've only had burrata a couple times before, but I remember each occasion as though it were a momentous event, and I know I'll remember this night, too.

I open my eyes—yes, I closed my eyes to savor it—and find Josh staring at me.

"What?" I ask.

"I admit I'm so uncultured that I thought burrata was a cured meat, rather than a cheese that can make a woman re-enact the diner scene from *When Harry Met Sally*."

I'm horrified at the thought of other people hearing my sexy burrata-induced noises. "I hope I wasn't *that* bad."

His eyes are heavy-lidded, and he trails his finger from the top of my knee-high boots up to my inner thigh. I'm practically overcome with sensation. There's the food, and his touch, and the beautiful surroundings…

"May I have some burrata?" he asks.

"Go ahead."

He tries a small amount with lavash and a roasted beet. He, too, moans when he pops it in his mouth.

"You see?" I say. "This stuff is magic." I have some more. Just a teeny-tiny bite—I'm going to make this last.

"I hope to hear you make those noises in my bed later," he whispers huskily, his gaze holding mine, a question in his eyes.

"Yes." The word comes out unsteadily. Not because I'm uncertain, but because I'm overwhelmed.

He gives me a slow, sexy smile.

"You clean up nice," I say, gesturing to his suit.

"Not like you. You're so fucking sexy, Sarah."

It doesn't sound ridiculous when he says that. Here, far above the city streets and the lake, life is just a touch surreal, and I believe him. The lights in the restaurant are low, but not so low that you can't read the menu and get a good look at your food… or the man sitting across from you.

I squeeze my thighs together. I'm looking forward to the rest of my food, but I'm also looking forward to later.

He watches me intently with his dark eyes, and my skin feels like it's exploding with awareness. I turn my attention back to my burrata, which looks damn fine, but nowhere near as fine as Josh.

The main course arrives soon after we finish our appetizers. My seared elk loin is exquisite, and the root vegetables that accompany it are cooked in a delicious amount of butter. Josh has the duck, which is very good, too—he lets me try some—but I'm partial to my elk.

You know when you order a meal and then, even if it's pretty good, you regret it because your dining partner's food is even better?

Well, I'm not having any regrets tonight.

I feed Josh a bite of my elk with cherry reduction. I manage not to stab him, which I count as a win.

"It's amazing, isn't it?" I say.

"Yes. Amazing."

His intensity tonight is different from usual. Usually he's more relaxed and friendly, but tonight, he has the super-rich, suit-wearing CEO thing going on.

I don't think he's unhappy with this meal, though; I don't see how anyone could be unhappy with it. Rather, I have the impression he's impatient to get me alone.

When I lick the cherry reduction off my fork and place it on top of my empty plate, he says, "Let's have dessert back at my place."

That's such a line, but it causes a pleasant hum in my body.

However, as much as I'm looking forward to going home with him...

"Not a chance," I say. "Nothing is getting in the way of me having dessert at Loren's. Not even you."

Everything on the dessert menu looks amazing, but my brain isn't functioning well enough to decide what to order. It's just screaming, *Sex! Sex!*

Then I see what's at the bottom of the menu, and I burst into laughter. "They have a hazelnut chocolate tart with cherries. We have to get it."

We order the tart, as well as a scoop of bananas foster ice cream. They're both heavenly.

I smile and swipe a piece of the tart crust off his lip. This time, unlike the day I first met him, I think it's an appropriate thing to do. It's not like we're strangers anymore.

"Your chocolate hazelnut tart is better," Josh says.

"That's sweet of you to say, but you don't need to."

My expert, objective opinion? This one is better.

"No, really," he says. "This is very good, but not as good as yours. You're amazingly talented." He says it with such conviction that I can't protest.

Pride bursts in my chest.

I know I'm good at what I do, but it's rare for someone I care about to compliment me like that, and Josh has done it more than once.

Yes, I care about him.

In the past decade, I haven't really been close to anyone in Toronto, and I'm not going to lie, my feelings for him scare me a little. But for now, I manage to push that aside and focus on the wonderful night we're having together.

I want to feel his skin against me; I want to feel him inside me. I want to spend the night in his bed and wake up next to him.

I want it *now*.

However, there are still two heavenly desserts sitting between us. I'm not leaving those half-finished, no matter how much I want Josh. It would be a sin to let them go to waste, but rather than savoring them slowly, I pick up the pace.

"What's the rush?" he asks.

"I want to get out of here." I wink at him.

I'm out of practice when it comes to flirtation and seduction. Those aren't skills that I spent any time developing in my adult life. So I suspect my wink doesn't look nearly as sexy as I want it to, but still, Josh's eyes darken, and he, too, starts eating quickly.

"I'm glad to hear it," he murmurs.

"I am most *intrigued* by the idea of putting something *scrumptious* in my mouth."

"Sarah," he says warningly.

"What? You want me to stop referencing that unfortunate email?"

He groans, then leans forward. "Well, yes. But I also want you to stop making me harder than I already am."

I actually shudder at that, despite the warmth of the restaurant.

Ten minutes later, we're in the back of the car he hired, heading uptown. Though traffic in Toronto is generally crappy, on Sunday night at nine o'clock, the roads aren't bad, and I'm not growling in impatience.

Besides, Josh is kissing me.

His hands stay above my shoulders, but the things he can do with his mouth...my God. I can't wait to feel his mouth between my legs. I have no doubt that he intends to go down on me and treat me very, very well.

We stumble into his house. He tears off my jacket and hat, then his own winter clothes, and starts kissing me again, his hands going to my neck to undo the bow at the back of my halter dress. After unclasping my strapless bra, he fills his hands with my breasts and brushes his thumb over my nipple.

I feel like I'm not quite myself. I, Sarah Winters, do not go on dates to fancy restaurants, then have a very attractive CEO devour me at his house in Forest Hill. Nor do I wear knee-high boots; rather, I keep them at the back of the closet and wonder why I ever bought them.

And yet.

I do feel like myself when I'm with him. I feel desired for who I am.

I'm not just some woman to Josh.

I'm Sarah Winters, and who I am matters to him.

This isn't just a one-night stand.

He pulls my dress over my head and rests his hands on my hips, at the top of my lacy black underwear, which I specifically wore because I intended to have sex tonight.

"You're so beautiful," he breathes. "I love the boots. The underwear." He gestures at me. "Everything. Everything about you tonight. I can't believe I was forced to eat bananas foster ice cream first."

"Poor baby. You had to eat ice cream."

He slides the tips of his fingers into my panties. "I want to do everything to you, but you can stop me at any time, okay?"

I nod, and he slides his hand lower.

We both groan as he brushes his finger over my slit.

"God, you're so wet."

"How could I not be when…"

I can't finish my sentence. He's pushing his finger inside me, and it's been so long since a man touched me intimately like this…and yet I don't think a man has ever touched me quite like *this*.

Needing to feel his skin, I start unbuttoning his shirt, my clumsy fingers not working as quickly as I want. When he grazes my clit, I have to stop what I'm doing, leaving his shirt half undone so I can grasp his shoulders for support.

He kisses my mouth as he touches me, and his other hand goes to my breast, massaging it, drawing the nipple to a tight peak. His mouth shifts to my breast, just for a moment, and then he's dropping to his knees and grinning wickedly up at me.

He pushes aside the gusset of my lacy underwear and puts his mouth on me. He licks over my slit, then slides his finger back in as he sucks on my clit.

I gasp and reach in desperation for something to hold on to—the doorknob in one hand and his hair in the other. He keeps pleasuring me, one hand grabbing my ass and keeping me against his face.

I can feel it coming, and then my orgasm washes over me like a tidal wave. It's nothing like the orgasms I occasionally give myself at night; it's so much more.

I breathe shakily and cry out before sliding down the door until I'm sitting on my ass, Josh between my legs.

"I've wanted to do that for so long," he murmurs.

He unzips and removes my boots, and it's a relief to finally be out of them. I wiggle my toes before he removes my underwear.

I'm naked before him.

He shudders as he rakes his gaze over me, and a part of me can't believe I'm causing a man like Josh Yu to respond like this.

Yet at the same time, it feels right to be naked with him.

Maybe we're going to do it here, in the front hall, the hard marble floor beneath my back...or my knees. However he wants is fine with me.

But instead, he scoops me up in his arms as though I weigh nothing and walks up the stairs. "I want to make love to you in my bed."

He enters the bedroom and deposits me on his bed, which is huge and covered in soft blankets. He climbs in next to me and makes quick work of his suit and boxers. And okay, I might drool the first time I see him in the nude, the first time I properly get a look at all his sculpted muscles.

I squirm against the bed as he positions himself over me, his gaze intent on my body. He's breathtaking, and I want him more than I've ever wanted another man.

Before this, I knew what it was like to have a need I had to satisfy, but I didn't know what it was like to want one particular person only, because nobody else would do.

I am in over my head, and all I can do is *want*.

"Are you ready?" he asks, reaching into his bedside table.

"Yes," I say. "*Yes*."

He chuckles low, and it vibrates in my chest.

I continue to squirm as he rolls on a condom. He notches the tip of his erection against my entrance and slowly pushes inside. I watch as he enters me, gasping when he's maybe halfway in.

"I'm sorry," I say. "It's been a while, and I—"

"Don't apologize for anything." He puts his finger to my mouth, then presses a kiss to my temple and kisses his way down my jaw and throat. So tenderly, even though I'm sure he's aching to be fully inside me.

I'm about to tell him to continue when he pushes in further, as though he can read my mind. Finally, he's seated within me, and I exhale slowly. He's so hard, and just the perfect size.

God, he feels amazing.

He brushes the hair back from my face. "Okay?"

I nod, and he rocks his hips, moving in and out of me with long strokes. I grip his back with my hands, feeling his muscles as he thrusts inside me.

"That's good," I say breathlessly. "Yes. Good."

If he likes dirty talk, too bad for him. I'm barely able to form words at all.

Some other time, perhaps. I know this will happen more than once.

One of his arms supports his weight, and he touches me with his other hand, as though worshipping me, as though every inch of my body is a work of art. Then he moves his hand between my legs, and my eyes pop open.

"Do you like that?" he asks.

I nod.

"Can you come again for me like this?"

"Yes," I whisper.

He stops thrusting, but his hand remains between my legs, rubbing light circles over my clit. "I have to stop. I don't want...to finish yet."

I'm glad that he, too, is overcome.

I love being joined with him like this. I tighten my hold on him and bring his chest against mine, skin against skin, and it feels glorious. When he starts moving again, I grind against him, and I can feel myself getting closer and closer.

"Josh," I say, my fingernails digging into his back, and then I come apart beneath him.

He growls as he spends himself inside me.

Afterward, he goes to the washroom to clean up, and I stay in the bed, rolling around in in the soft sheets. They feel so luxurious against my sensitized skin, and I can't help grinning.

When he returns to bed, he wraps his arms around me from behind and presses kisses all over my neck and shoulder. "I hope you have no plans to go anywhere."

"Of course not."

I often leave after sex, but tonight, it's not a consideration. I will stay here with him.

"I promise to last more than two minutes next time," he says. "I was just…you know."

Yes, I do know.

I turn in his arms. We kiss lazily; it's perfection. I run my hands through his short hair and over the light stubble on his jaw, and he runs his hands over my curves.

I want to be in his bed, with his arms around me, for as long as I can.

WHEN MY ALARM goes off at six o'clock, I turn it off, then roll over and see Sarah next to me in bed. She's scribbling in a little purple notebook.

I smile at her. "Morning. How long have you been up?"

"An hour. I usually wake up at five, even on my day off."

"What are you writing?"

"Notes on the hazelnut chocolate tart we ate last night. I didn't intend to do any work, but I have a couple ideas for minor changes I can make to my chocolate hazelnut tarts."

"Should I be insulted you were paying enough attention to your food last night that you can make *notes* on it?"

She laughs. I love hearing her laugh first thing in the morning. It's good to wake up with her in my bed.

I toss the notebook to the floor and roll on top of her and kiss her. We're both wearing short-sleeve Henleys—I lent her one of mine—and underwear and nothing else, but it's too much clothing. I love feeling her softness beneath me, and I ache to touch her skin.

I'm about to reach for the bottom of her shirt when I notice a book on her pillow.

A Secret Baby for the CEO.

I freeze when I read the title.

Sarah sees where I'm looking and tosses the book on the floor next to the notebook. "Just some reading I was doing before you got up. One of my employees decided to give me a bunch of romances about CEOs since I was going on a date with you."

"Right."

A Secret Baby for the CEO. The book is face-down on the floor, but the title keeps running through my head.

I roll back to the other side of the bed.

This isn't the morning-after I anticipated. I imagined waking up together and fooling around, cocooned together in my room, safe from the winter cold, then going downstairs, where I'd make her breakfast. Maybe we'd have a shower together.

I usually get to work around seven thirty but figured I would show up late today, at nine or—gasp!—ten o'clock.

But now I'm thinking about what happened when I was sixteen.

"What's a secret baby?" I ask.

"The CEO got the heroine pregnant, but she didn't realize it until after they'd broken up. She kept the baby a secret from him for a couple years, until they happened to meet again... Josh, what's wrong?"

I feel like the details of my past are something I owe Sarah, like it's a big secret I shouldn't be keeping from her.

I turn toward her and prop my head up on my hand.

She does the same. "I hope you're not assuming that I'm already dreaming about marriage and babies with you and—"

"I got my girlfriend pregnant when I was sixteen. That's why my dad doesn't talk to me."

She's quiet for a moment, seemingly disoriented by the change in conversation, then reaches out and strokes my cheek. I lean into her caress. I'm not used to people touching me like this, and it feels nice.

It feels nice because it's Sarah who's doing it.

"Is there…" She hesitates. "Your girlfriend—did she have the baby?"

I shake my head. "I'd have a teenage kid right now if she had. I can't imagine it. And if he or she also had a kid at sixteen, I'd be a grandfather."

I start to climb out of bed, but Sarah grabs my hand.

"Did you tell your father? How did he find out?"

I hadn't planned on sharing everything, but it pours out of me. "My girlfriend told her sister, because she wanted her sister to drive her to the doctor—we were so young that we only had our learner's permits. Her sister told her parents, who were friends with my parents, and…yeah. Her parents accused me of corrupting and pressuring their daughter, since I was the rebel, and she was the straight A-plus student. But she wanted to have sex as much as I did, and it was only once that we were stupid and didn't use a condom. We were confused about a lot of things and thought she couldn't get pregnant at that time of month, and…it happened."

I pause to take a breath. I'm not sure why I'm telling her all this, but I can't help it.

"To my dad," I continue, "being bad was getting a B or missing curfew once. Getting a girl pregnant was beyond his comprehension. He didn't understand how that could happen to his son, and he was furious with me because my mom's health wasn't great at the time and I made her worry."

"And you've been paying for that for almost twenty years?"

I nod.

"Oh, Josh."

She pulls me into her arms, and I'm caught off-guard by her reaction. Not many people know this story, and I'm not used to someone comforting me after I tell it.

"Melinda and I," I say, my voice hoarse, "our relationship didn't survive the aftermath, but we're friends now. Not close friends, but she lives in Toronto, too. She's an OB/GYN who's a crusader for quality sex ed. What we had in school wasn't great, and—"

"Your parents didn't talk to you about it?"

I bark out a laugh. "Ha! No way."

"My mom did. She was good with that stuff." Sarah frowns, then shakes her head. "Not that she approved of casual sex, and not that I was having sex in high school, but I had all the knowledge I needed. I know many kids don't get that at home, which is why it's important for it to be part of the curriculum. I'm sorry about your father. I'm sorry he let that one incident destroy your relationship."

"If I hadn't been so stupid…"

"You were a kid who was careless once. You didn't do anything malicious. Lots of people deal with an unplanned pregnancy at one point or another, whether or not they use birth control."

"It wasn't just that. For two years, I was a nightmare for my parents."

"You told me what you were like. It reminded me of my brother, but my parents never would have stopped talking to him, not for more than a day. Now he's an auto mechanic with a wife and two kids, and he has a good relationship with both of my parents." She puts her hand on my shoulder. "Josh, it seems like you've been angry at yourself for seventeen years, but you're a good guy. Truly. The fact that he doesn't talk to you is on him, not you, and he's missing out. No matter what happens with your family on Pi Day, you're okay." She gives me a kind smile. "I had a great time last night."

"And now I'm burdening you with my past. It's just…when I saw the title of that book, it felt like I was keeping a big secret from you." God, I'm making a hash of this.

I feel uncomfortably vulnerable, even though she's reassuring me. A man who has a successful company and friends and a house in Forest Hill shouldn't need to be told he's okay, but I did need to hear that.

I hold her close and pepper her skin with kisses. We stay in bed, snuggling, for a few minutes.

To be honest, this isn't something I've done much of. I have one-night stands, I have flings, and often we wake up beside each other, but we don't just hold each other.

I haven't had a girlfriend since Melinda. I told myself I wasn't interested, and besides, I was busy with work. I was always clear about this from the beginning—I never led a woman on—and if we started feeling too close, I'd break it off.

But being here with Sarah feels pretty damn awesome, and I'm starting to wonder...was I punishing myself? Did I think I didn't deserve to have a relationship after what happened when I was sixteen, after I disappointed my parents, after all the crap Melinda had to put up with in the aftermath?

Perhaps.

And for once, I think this time might be different. Maybe I could have a proper relationship with Sarah and wake up to her scribbling recipe notes and reading romance novels in my bed on a regular basis.

Maybe I could have that, and maybe I deserve it.

Her stomach rumbles.

"Let me make you breakfast," I say.

"What are you offering?"

"I can prepare a few very fine breakfasts. All begin with coffee. How do you like yours?"

"A little cream, a little sugar."

"Very classy. Alright, option one. The first course is a glass of refreshing orange juice, followed by a bowl of O-shaped cereal with cold two-percent milk, fresh from...um, Loblaws. The cereal comes in two flavors: our finest chocolate, or honey nut, the honey produced by cartoon bumblebees."

She giggles. "Are you offering me Chocolate or Honey Nut Cheerios?"

"I am, but wait until you hear option two."

"I'm listening."

"Option two—which can also include orange juice, if you desire—is a bowl of frosted oats and marshmallow shapes. The exciting thing about this option? There are now unicorn marshmallows."

"Lucky Charms?"

"You are correct."

"I didn't know they had unicorns."

I shake my head. "Tsk-tsk. I thought you were a food expert."

"I can't believe you have Lucky Charms and Chocolate Cheerios."

Okay, I'm starting to feel a bit embarrassed that my breakfast choices are the kind a seven-year-old would make.

"There's also a third option," I say. "Toast with peanut butter and jam. A rarely-chosen option in this household, but it does exist."

"No, I'll go with option one."

"Chocolate or honey nut?"

"Chocolate, please."

We've moved on from talking about my past to talking about Lucky Charms and Chocolate Cheerios, and somehow, it all seems perfectly normal and natural and wonderful.

Twenty minutes later, we're sitting at my kitchen table. Usually I'd be flipping through emails or reading the news on my phone while I eat breakfast, but today, I have company.

Sarah's still wearing one of my Henleys and her underwear, but nothing else. A very good situation indeed, and one I plan to take advantage of later, but for now, we're drinking our coffee and eating our cereal together.

I scoop up a unicorn marshmallow with my spoon and deposit it in Sarah's bowl of Chocolate Cheerios.

"A unicorn for you, my lady," I say.

"How kind of you, Sir CEO."

"Sir CEO? Is that what the heroine calls the hero in the book you're reading?"

"Well, I haven't gotten very far, and mostly she's been calling him 'you asshole.'"

I chuckle. "Does this asshole eat Lucky Charms for breakfast?"

"No."

I gasp in faux horror. "The author didn't do her research. CEOs *always* eat Lucky Charms for breakfast. It's the source of our power."

We giggle stupidly together. It's amazing how much fun talking nonsense can be when you're doing it with the right person. Sarah's light brown hair is a bit of a mess and some of her makeup from last night is smudged under her eyes, but she's not self-conscious about it, and she looks beautiful.

She sips her coffee. "And what power would that be?"

"Our power to, uh, look devastatingly sexy in suits and yell at people all day?"

"You don't seem like the yelling type."

"I'm not."

"And you don't wear suits to work. Although you did wear one last night, and you did look devastatingly sexy in it."

"It's all thanks to Lucky Charms." I pat my abs.

She snorts, and when I not-so-discreetly slide up the bottom of my shirt, she can't seem to tear her gaze away.

"You spend lots of time in kitchens," I say. "You must have had sex in a kitchen at some point?"

"Absolutely not."

"No?"

"It's unhygienic. I keep my kitchen spotless."

"Fortunately, I'm not as strict about my kitchen." I'm finished eating, but she's still got a small amount of cereal in her bowl, and in the time it takes her to eat it, I intend to drive her crazy. I shift my chair close to hers and slide my finger up her inner thigh to the edge of her underwear. "I say we change your record. Today, you're having sex in my kitchen. Sound like a plan?"

She nods, as though unable to speak while I'm touching her like this.

"Where would you like me to fuck you?" I ask.

Her pupils dilate at that word, and I file that away for future use. Last night, there wasn't much talking; mostly it was me checking in with her, making sure everything was good for her as I tried not to blow my load too soon.

I want to learn everything she likes.

"Perhaps on the table," I say casually as I slide my fingers inside the crotch of her panties. "Your body spread out like a buffet before me. Or maybe you'd like to sit on the counter, gripping the edge of it as I thrust into you over and over?" I slip the tip of one finger inside her. She's getting wet, and I suppress a groan. "Or perhaps you'd prefer to be fucked from behind against the fridge?"

Her breath quickens.

"Okay, against the fridge it is." I take off her panties and slip two fingers all the way inside her. "Good?"

When she nods, I kiss her lips as I stroke her, relishing her reaction to me. I pluck the unicorn marshmallow out of the bowl with my other hand and place it on her tongue.

"There," I whisper. "Now you have special powers, too."

"What powers do I have?"

"The power to drive me absolutely mad." I press a kiss to her neck. "Actually, scratch that. You were already driving me mad."

I slide to the floor in front of her chair and part her legs. I lick her clit and her eyes flutter closed, and when I curl my finger inside her, they pop open again.

"Maybe the unicorn marshmallow gave you the power to have ten orgasms in a row."

"Ten orgasms? I'd be a heap on the floor afterward."

"Hmm." I lift my head. "Is that a challenge?"

She pushes my head back between her legs, and I laugh softly as I set about giving the best oral sex of my life. I usually pride myself at being great at going down on a woman, but I'm determined that this time will be even better. I want the very best for Sarah, who eats both burrata at fine restaurants and sugary cereal at breakfast with me.

If a woman stays the night, I always offer her breakfast, but not Lucky Charms. My love of Lucky Charms isn't the sort of thing I want the women who sleep with me to know, but Sarah is special. Even though she makes the world's finest pies, Sarah has learned about my not-so-classy breakfast choices.

I give her a long lick, and she clutches my hair, holding me against her. Not that I'm going anywhere. She tastes magnificent. I love having my face buried between her legs. Love being surrounded by her body, her scent.

My dick is almost painfully hard, but I ignore it and keep touching Sarah. Her soft little moans are like music, and when she cries out and shakes as she reaches her climax, I smile against her in satisfaction.

I stand up and pull off my shirt and boxers. She rakes her gaze over me, her eyes hungry.

Good.

I circle my arms around her and walk her backward until she hits the fridge. Her mouth widens in surprise. A few magnets and papers fall to the floor, but I don't care.

"Did you think I was kidding about doing it against the fridge?" I grin.

"I…I didn't know what to think."

"Think about how good I'm going to make you feel. Again and again." I turn her around so she's facing the fridge, and I slide my fingers inside her once more. She's still so wet for me, and I can't wait to get inside her.

"Josh," she says.

I roll on the condom that I tucked into my waistband and push myself inside her. All in one thrust, unlike last night.

Christ, she feels amazing.

I wrap my arm around her chest to hold her up, and I slip my other hand between her legs to touch her clit. I kiss her neck as I begin to move inside her, lost in the feel of her. Her back against my chest, the weight of her breasts above my arm, her tight wetness around my cock.

"You like being fucked like this, darling?" The endearment comes unconsciously.

She nods helplessly.

I nuzzle her neck and bite her skin, the opposite side from where I gave her a hickey last week.

"Oh, God. Oh, God," she whispers.

I push inside her again and again, and when her chest slams against the fridge, sending another magnet skittering across the floor, she cries out.

I can't remember the last time I felt so lost in a woman.

Actually, I don't think it's ever happened before.

I slam into her harder, her cries spurring me on, and then she goes rigid for a moment and cries out even louder than before.

"Sarah," I groan as I follow her over the edge.

When I pull out of her, we collapse together on the cold tile of the kitchen floor. I hold her in my arms, because I need to. I *need* to feel her skin against mine and to keep her with me.

Usually once I've slept with a woman a couple times, I start worrying that she'll want more of me than I'm capable of giving.

Not today, though.

I think I might be capable of it, and perhaps I told myself

otherwise because I believed I didn't deserve it. I won't rush into anything, but I'm not going to pull back, and I don't regret telling her more than I've told all the other women I've slept with.

"So this is what happens when you have Chocolate Cheerios or Lucky Charms for breakfast," Sarah murmurs. "I should do it more often."

I laugh and press a kiss to her temple.

"What time is it?" she asks.

I look at the microwave. "Seven thirty. I'm usually at the office by now."

"I'm sorry for throwing off your schedule. Except I'm totally not."

"It's no problem. I was more than happy to introduce you to kitchen sex."

"Mm. I suppose I do enjoy kitchen sex after all."

"You more than enjoyed it," I say. "It blew your mind."

"You're a little full of yourself."

"Are you saying I'm wrong?"

"Not at all."

I run my hand down her side. "Do you live near Happy As Pie? I'll drive you home when I go to the office."

"You can drive? You don't just pay a chauffeur to be at your beck and call?" she teases.

"Last night was just for you." And then I repeat myself, my tone serious this time. I want her to know I really do mean it. "Just for you."

She smiles at me. "It's rush hour. Traffic will be better if we wait an hour and a half, maybe two hours, and there are lots of things we could do in two hours."

"I like the way you think."

I sweep her into my arms and carry her upstairs.

∾

I walk into the office at ten o'clock, whistling.

Clarissa jumps up from her desk. "Josh. Thank God. I was worried. You never come in later than eight. What happened?"

"Oh, nothing," I say airily. "Just, uh…had some errands to run."

"Right. Okay. You've had two calls—"

"Josh!" It's Amrita. "Can I talk to you for a moment?" She pulls me into her office without waiting for a response.

"What is it?" I ask. "It sounds urgent."

She smirks. "So, did you prove to Sarah that the ramen incident didn't do any permanent damage? That's why you're late, isn't it?"

"What ramen… Oh. *Oh.* I can't believe you brought that up on Saturday."

"But it didn't hurt your chances with her, did it? No harm done, then. I even heard you whistling a minute ago. Must have been good."

"I didn't whistle!"

"Haha, very funny." She pauses. "You really like her, don't you?"

"I do."

And I'm going to be thinking about her all day.

WHEN JOSH DROPS me off at my apartment, I head inside and collapse on my couch. I squeeze a pillow to my chest, a goofy grin on my face.

That was the best date of my life, no question. The wonderful restaurant! The sex! Breakfast! Josh and I can be serious or playful together—though more often it's the latter—and it's all good. I'm not used to being with a man in so many different ways like that.

And now I have the whole day off! I'm meeting Chloe and Valerie at Baldwin Street Sushi at noon, but until then, I have no plans.

I change out of my halter dress, thinking about how I was a different person when I put it on yesterday, and then I make myself a cup of tea and settle back on the couch with *A Secret Baby for the CEO*.

~

"Dude must have a magic penis," Valerie says. "That's the only explanation."

I nearly spit out my tea. "What?"

"Please excuse Valerie. She tends to make inappropriate comments." Chloe leans toward me and says in a hushed tone, "Well? Does he?"

"Um," I say.

"You look really happy and relaxed," Valerie says. "Almost like you're glowing. So it must have been an awesome date."

"Yeah, it was pretty great."

"When did you get home?"

"Nine thirty this morning. He drove me home on the way to work."

"I knew it." Valerie slaps the table. "There was definitely sex."

I study the list of lunch specials, my cheeks heating.

"There's no need to be ashamed," Chloe says, putting her hand on my shoulder. "Three-date rules and all that—it's nonsense."

"I'm not ashamed I slept with him. I'm just not used to talking about men. At all. And I rarely date." I'm also not used to going out for lunch with friends.

"I don't date, either," Valerie says. "Men are dicks. At least, that's a common theme with the men in my life."

The waitress comes around and we place our orders. I get a maki special with salmon and California rolls.

"Where did Josh take you for dinner last night?" Chloe asks.

I tell them about Loren's and all the amazing food, and I'm practically drooling by the time our miso soup arrives.

I also tell them about the large stack of CEO romances that Ann gave me, and how Josh caught me reading *A Secret Baby for the CEO* this morning, which sends Valerie into uncontrollable laughter.

But I don't tell them what Josh told me after seeing that book, of course. I still can't believe his father has held it against him for so long. Hopefully the Pi Day party will make a difference. At least his dad is coming—that's a good first step.

"Guess what Josh ate for breakfast today," I say.

"The blood and sweat of his employees?" Valerie suggests.

"Oh, Val." Chloe gives her a look. "Bacon and eggs? Oatmeal? Toast?"

Valerie shakes her head. "It can't be anything quite so boring, or Sarah wouldn't have said anything about it."

"Lucky Charms," I say. "He eats Lucky Charms for breakfast."

Valerie sips her miso soup. "How sophisticated."

"He claims all CEOs do. He says it's the source of their, uh, powers."

"Powers in bed?" Chloe asks. "Which marshmallow gives him those powers?"

"Maybe there are marshmallow dicks in Lucky Charms now," Valerie says. "Which give men the power to be giant dicks in business and have big dicks in the bedroom."

"Wait a second," I say. "Are we seriously talking about marshmallow dicks?"

"Sure, why not? It's a perfectly normal conversation. They do exist, you know. You can find anything on Amazon. I came across them the other day."

"I'm almost scared to ask," Chloe says, "but what were you searching for that resulted in you stumbling upon marshmallow dicks on Amazon?"

Valerie shrugs. "Who knows. I don't remember anymore."

The wheels in my mind are turning. Perhaps I could buy a package of these marshmallow dicks and sneak them into Josh's box of Lucky Charms.

I cover my mouth to stifle my laughter.

God, I just want to keep laughing today. I had a great date last night, and I'm making friends who talk about marshmallow dicks while eating sushi, and all is well with the world.

≈

"Shit!" I pull the pan of hazelnuts out of the oven. They're burnt. I'll have to toss them.

If only I could do anything right in the kitchen today.

The kitchen is my home, and I'm usually...well, maybe not invincible in my home, but quite competent.

I don't feel competent right now.

Fatima comes over and examines the pan. "Those don't look good."

I almost snap at her and say, *No, really*. But I bite my tongue.

I finish the spiced apple pie filling while I toast another batch of hazelnuts, which I manage not to burn, and start chopping dark chocolate. I'm making another attempt at chocolate hazelnut tarts today.

Okay, I can do this. I am going to make the best damn tarts in the world, and Josh is going to take one bite and ask me to marry him—as a joke, obviously—and then he's going to kiss me senseless.

It's such a pleasure to be hugged and kissed by him. The sex is amazing, but the other intimacies, the ones that don't lead directly to sex, are amazing, too. Just lying in bed with someone in the morning—that felt like such a luxury. Whenever I'm not at work, I'm usually alone, and it was nice to be with someone else. To be with *him*.

Nobody has ever made me feel the way he does.

I'm not in love with Josh, though. That's ridiculous. I didn't meet him very long ago, and we only had our first kiss last week. Of course I'm not in love with him.

But it's starting to happen. I'm falling for him.

I've been thinking about him all damn day. I've been thinking about his scent, his taste...the way it feels to thrust my fingers through his hair when he has his head between my legs...the way it feels when he looks at me as though I'm the sexiest woman he's ever seen.

Yes. Me. I'm—

"Ahhhh!" I shriek, dropping my knife. "Fuck."

I usually don't scream obscenities at work, but then again, I don't usually burn hazelnuts and cut my finger open.

"Are you okay?" Fatima rushes over.

I grab a paper towel and press it to the wound. It's not actually a bad cut. Bloody, but not deep. "I'll be fine."

Unfortunately, I'll have to throw out the chocolate I was chopping, since I bled all over it.

What the hell is wrong with me today?

Well, that's pretty obvious. It's Josh Yu. He's making me lose my focus—and I'm usually pretty good at focusing on Happy As Pie.

But now, instead of thinking about chocolate tarts and apple pies, I'm thinking about cuddling and kissing and meaningful looks…and the man with the greatest smile in the world.

I exhale slowly, then head to the washroom to clean myself up and bandage my finger.

I need to make some ground rules for myself. I cannot afford to be so distracted.

First of all, I won't think about Josh when I'm at work. Well, I'll only think of him in a business sense—I'll think about making awesome food for his party, and the logistics. When I'm at Happy As Pie, Josh is not a man I'm dating, but a client. No mooning over his smile. No remembering how he fucked me against his fridge yesterday morning.

I feel a rush of heat between my legs, but I force my mind to think about more appropriate things. I cannot afford to keep burning food and cutting myself.

Second of all, I will not change my work schedule for him. I will work just as many hours as I did before, and I will not text him during the workday.

On my own time, I can do whatever I want, but I refuse to let a man compromise my dream, which I've worked so hard to achieve.

I take a few more deep breaths before heading back to the kitchen.

I can do this.

I RUN my finger over the cream-colored envelope. My address is printed in a fussy script.

I know exactly what this is. I've been expecting it.

I open the envelope, and sure enough, there's a wedding invitation inside. It's edged with pink and red flowers, and the Chinese character for "double happiness" is in red at the top, followed by the names.

Melinda Leung and Terrence Chu.

I lay the invitation down on the kitchen table. There's a strange pressure in my chest, but it's not jealousy. It's not regret.

I'm happy for Melinda. I only wish good things for her, but it's tinged with…I don't know what. Maybe it *is* regret. Not regret that we broke up, but regret that she's had a number of boyfriends since high school, and I've just had a bunch of meaningless flings, nothing that resembled a relationship.

Until Sarah.

I scrub my hands down my face. I have no idea how to be *more* for a woman, no idea how I'm supposed to act. When I was sixteen, it was completely different. I was in high school; I couldn't even drive.

I loved Melinda. Not the deep kind of love that I'm sure her fiancé has for her now, but I loved her in the way I was capable of at the time. I used to walk her home and carry her textbooks, and I'd pull her behind trees and kiss her every five minutes. I saved my money so I could take her out for pizza and burgers, rather than spending it on weed. I bought her pretty hair clips. I sent her cutesy emails and had long phone conversations with her; there were no smartphones when we were in high school. We'd talk on ICQ, though.

And then...

I grip the table, then exhale slowly.

It's okay. It was a long time ago. But I feel guilty about the position I put her in. Her big-mouth sister told everyone at school, and Melinda had to deal with endless comments behind her back, slut-shaming from her friends. She nearly switched schools.

Her parents must no longer think I'm a hellion—if they hated me, I wouldn't be invited.

If only her parents could convince my father of that.

I set the invitation aside. I don't want to look at it anymore. It's about a future wedding, but to me, it represents the past, and I'm trying to move forward. I'm trying to tell myself I deserve another chance at this. It's ridiculous that something from seventeen years ago still haunts me, yet I can't get around the fact that it's the reason my father doesn't talk to me.

But I'm trying to change that, too.

I'll be good to Sarah, I swear. I'm just not entirely sure how to do it.

I'm a rich man. Not a super-crazy powerful wealthy man, but I'm not lacking for anything. I don't need to save my money for a slice at the slightly-nicer pizza chain. I can take Sarah out to fancy places, like I did on Sunday night. I can buy her pretty things.

I'm about to do a little searching on my phone when I get a

text from Sarah. Just seeing her name on my phone makes my blood pump faster.

She's sent me a selfie, taken from an awkward angle, of her about to take a bite of a chocolate tart. I laugh. It's a silly picture, and I like it very much. Cute and sexy, even though she wasn't trying to be sexy—but I always think she's sexy.

My new chocolate hazelnut tart, she says. *It's even better than the last one.*

That's hard to believe, because the last one was pretty damn spectacular, but I'll take her word for it.

I want to see you tomorrow, I text. After staring at that picture, I'm overwhelmed with the need to see her, but it's already eight o'clock—I got home late—so I don't ask to see her right now. *Maybe try that chocolate hazelnut tart.*

No, not tomorrow. I'm busy. Thursday? We can do something for dinner.

Sure. Thursday dinner it is.

Hopefully she'll come over afterward. I want to take her to bed again, and maybe feed her some of that chocolate hazelnut tart myself. Lick the crumbs from her lips.

God, I was really hoping to see her tomorrow, but Thursday will have to do.

However, when four o'clock rolls around on Wednesday afternoon, I decide I can't wait another day. I need to see her now, even if it's just for a few minutes.

I leave the office early and walk through the slushy streets to Happy As Pie, wondering if she's been thinking about me as much as I've been thinking about her.

MY UTERUS HATES ME.

Like, it really fucking hates me.

I should be in the kitchen, assembling chicken pot pies. Because of Josh's party, we have more to make than usual.

Instead, I'm in my tiny office, ostensibly doing financial stuff, but I'm making little progress.

There's another stab of pain, and I curl up in my chair.

My period wasn't supposed to start today. I thought I'd have until Friday. I thought I'd be able to have a nice date with Josh tomorrow without having to worry about it.

But it's only Wednesday, and I'm doubled over in pain.

Okay, Sarah. Come on. You can do it.

I remove my hand from my lower abdomen and scroll down with the mouse, but I don't understand what I'm seeing. The numbers are floating around on the screen. Normally, numbers make perfect sense to me, but not today.

Ahhhhhh.

Goddamn uterus. Why do you hate me so much?

There's a knock on the door, and Ann pops her head into my office. "Josh is here to see you," she says with a smile.

A moment later, Josh enters, closing the door behind him.

Our date isn't until tomorrow, right? Or has the pain screwed with my memory?

"Hey, Sarah." He smiles at me. He's wearing a blue Henley today, and he looks great.

Whereas I must look like complete shit.

If I were feeling better, I might think of jumping him right now. Instead, I'm thinking about how I can get rid of him as quickly as possible. I have work to do, and I'm in pain. The last thing I need is a surprise visit.

Though he really is nice to look at.

More stabbing pain.

"Oh, God," I whisper.

He kneels in front of my chair and put his hands on my knees. "What's wrong?"

"Not feeling well," I mumble, "but I'll be okay soon. Lots of work to do."

"You're pale." He reaches up to touch my forehead. "And you're sweating."

Yeah, that happens sometimes when I have cramps. At least my nausea isn't too bad.

"You shouldn't be working if you're sick," he says. "Let me call a cab and take you home. Or maybe I should take you to the doctor."

I shake my head. "Don't need a doctor. I'll be fine tomorrow, or Friday at the latest. I'm not sick, just...ahhhh."

I could tell him the truth, but talking about periods with a guy seems weird. I've never done it before. I suppose women with boyfriends and husbands must mention it to them at some point, but I haven't had close relationships like that, and if I had my period, I wouldn't be having a one-night stand, which is usually the situation when I go to bed with a guy.

Except Josh is different. Josh, the cause of my burnt hazelnuts and bleeding thumb yesterday. I was determined not to let him affect my work, and I arranged for our date to be a day later than he suggested so I could have some distance from him. Yet here he is in my office.

"You should have texted first," I say.

He frowns as he studies my face. I'm annoyed with him for this unexpected visit, and yet he looks so concerned that I can't really be mad at him. Plus, I'm in too much pain to be mad.

"Ughhh." I clutch my abdomen.

"I don't know how you can get any work done like this. It's four thirty. You might as well go home, although I really think you should see a doctor, and if it's contagious, you shouldn't be in the kitchen... *Oh*." He presses his lips together and nods. "You have cramps."

"Yes." I look down, mortified. Talking about this with anyone other than my mother or sister feels strange.

"Is there anything you can take? Painkillers? I can run to the pharmacy and get some."

"I already took ibuprofen," I say miserably. Most of the time, ibuprofen is enough to keep me functional for the two or three days of the month that I have cramps. But a couple times a year, my cramps are so bad that ibuprofen only takes the edge off. Barely.

Unfortunately, today is one of those times.

I rest my cheek on the back of the chair and release a shuddering breath. In and out. In and out. Breathe through the pain.

"Sarah." His hand is on my other cheek, stroking me tenderly. "Please. Let me take you home and look after you."

"I won't be any fun."

"You don't need to be fun. Can I shut off your computer and call a cab?"

"It's only a fifteen-minute walk. We don't need a cab."

He gives me a look.

"A fifteen-minute walk," I repeat. "I'll be able to walk...in just a minute. Maybe. I don't know."

He pulls out his phone and orders the cab from an app, I guess. I can barely pay attention to what's going on. Then he comes to the computer and saves and closes everything I have open before shutting it off.

I tell my employees that I'm leaving early because I'm not feeling well—the first time that's ever happened. When I'm finished, the cab is waiting, and Josh helps me inside. He sits next to me and wraps his arms around me as the cab lurches forward.

Dammit. Now I truly am nauseous. I hope I don't throw up. Though this is probably better than walking.

I mumble my address, then squeeze my eyes shut and lean on Josh's shoulder.

When we pull up to my apartment building a few minutes later, I manage to stumble inside and put the key in my door. Josh helps me into my bedroom, where I change into a pair of pajama pants and notice the small blood stain on my jeans. Crap. I collapse on my bed, curled up in a ball. Everything hurts and I'm still nauseous. Josh gets into bed and puts his hand on my side, and the concerned look on his face makes it even harder to breathe.

"Can I get you anything?" he asks.

"Hot water bottle."

I tell him where to find one. He gets up, and I hear him poking around in my kitchen. My instinct is to help him. He's a guest; I should be doing this. But getting up would be so much effort.

There's another stabbing pain, and I let out a string of curses. I haven't had cramps this bad in years.

Josh returns with the hot water bottle, two cups of tea, and a little plate of orange slices, strawberries, digestive cookies, and chocolate.

"I love you," I say, then my eyes open wide in terror.

Shit. I just told a guy that I love him.

He runs his hand down my arm, unperturbed by the words I

said far too soon. I think he understands that I was just thankful for what he's doing for me.

God, I'm such a mess right now.

He holds out a piece of chocolate, and I eat it from his fingers. *Oh, chocolate, I love you, too. You are so sweet and delicious and—*

"Ahhhh." Pain shoots through me.

I snuggle under the blankets and put my hot water bottle on my aching lower back. Josh wraps his arms around me. The way he touches me isn't sexual, but soothing and intimate, and for the next few minutes, he peppers me with kisses and feeds me fruit and chocolate.

"How are you doing now?" he asks.

I don't know how to answer. I'm in pain, but a man has never looked after me like this before, and it's nice. I wonder what I could have had, relationship-wise, in the past decade if I hadn't focused only on my career.

Lots of burnt hazelnuts and cut thumbs, perhaps.

Or maybe…

I move the hot water bottle to my front and turn over so I'm facing away from Josh. He immediately knows what I want and puts his arm around me from behind. I try to focus on his body pressed against my back rather than the pain I'm feeling. He kisses my temple, and God, it's so tender and sweet.

"I feel like runny caramel, spreading out over the bed," I say, then realize it sounds silly.

"I can't say I've ever felt like that before." But he doesn't tell me I'm silly.

I curl up into more of a ball. It hurts, it hurts so much, but Josh is holding me, caressing my hair and forehead, even though I'm disheveled and sweaty and not at my best. He's here for me, in whatever way I need him, and I feel like everything will be okay.

Eventually, the pain recedes enough for me to fall asleep.

When I wake up, it's dark except for the bright light of a screen. I blink, disoriented.

Josh is sitting up in bed, working on his laptop

My water bottle is lukewarm, and there's a cold cup of tea on the bedside table, plus a piece of chocolate and a digestive cookie.

"Hey," I say groggily.

He sets his laptop aside and pulls me against him. "How are you doing?"

"Better. Still not great, but much better."

The pain is dull and manageable now. Although with Josh, almost everything seems manageable. I'm stronger with him next to me.

I smile at him, and he runs his thumb over my lower lip.

My boobs feel weird. I frown, then realize I fell asleep with my bra on, a very unusual occurrence for me. I undo the clasp at the back, pull the bra out through my sleeve, and throw it on the ground.

Much better.

"Impressive." Josh pulls me into an embrace.

A part of me is amazed he's still here.

I guess that's what people do when they care about each other.

I don't want to think too much about where we're going, and for now, I'll just let myself enjoy the luxury of having him here. I rarely feel this crappy. I can have some time off.

"What do you want for dinner?" he asks. "I'll order us something."

Although I'm getting hungry, just the thought of deciding what to order is overwhelming.

"Whatever you want," I say.

"No, we'll have what *you* want. You're the one who's not feeling well."

"Too complicated…"

"Okay." He nods. "I'll figure it out. Is there anything you don't like?"

I shake my head. "I'm not picky."

"One more question: soup or fried food?"

"Soup."

Soup sounds delicious. I have cramps, and outside, it's a blustery winter day. The weather should be warming up soon, seeing as it's March, but it's still below freezing today.

"No problem." He pulls up a food delivery app on his phone. "This is one of the apps we developed."

I close my eyes and snuggle up under the covers as he figures out dinner. It's nice to have someone else to deal with things for me. I'm used to doing it all myself, both at home and when I'm at work.

But right now, I leave it to him, and I trust he'll get me something tasty.

"It'll be about forty-five minutes," he says. "I hope that's okay."

I nod and pop a cookie into my mouth.

We hang out in bed as we wait, me dozing in and out, Josh idly stroking my hair and working on his laptop. It's comfortable. I feel like we're an old married couple.

I jolt up at that thought. An old married couple?

"Something wrong?" he asks.

I shake my head and cocoon myself in the blankets.

When the food arrives, Josh goes to get it. He returns a few minutes later, scoops me up into his arms, and brings me to my small kitchen table, where the food is laid out. A plate of dumplings sits in the middle of the table, and he's poured the soup into two large bowls. There are green onions and cilantro sprinkled on top of wide noodles and broth and some kind of meat.

"It smells delicious," I say.

"Lamb and hand-pulled noodles."

I try a bite. When I groan in pleasure, Josh smiles.

"Is this what your mom made when you were sick?" I ask. "Like chicken noodle soup?"

He chuckles. "This food is from Shaanxi, one of the northern provinces in China. My family is from Hong Kong. Mom would make me jook—congee—with chicken and ginger."

Ah. Okay. I feel a little stupid.

I reach for a dumpling, which also contains lamb, not something I associate with Chinese cuisine, but clearly there is much I don't know.

"How are you feeling now?" he asks.

"Not too bad." I squeeze his leg. "Sorry I'm not any fun today."

"Sarah, you have to stop apologizing for that. I'm here because I want to be. It's far from a hardship to look after you, though I hate seeing you in pain."

"It's just...I feel like I always have to be 'on' when I'm with other people, you know? Except maybe my family. And I'm not 'on' right now."

"I can leave if you want, but—"

"No, no." A void opens up inside me at the thought. "It's nice. You can stay."

He smiles and squeezes my hand under the table, and we sit like that in companionable silence, eating our noodles and lamb.

My phone buzzes. I don't reach for it, but when it buzzes again, Josh hands it to me.

Are you okay?? Chloe asks. *I stopped by to see you and Ann said you went home sick.*

Cramps, I tell her, not in the mood for lying. *Josh is taking care of me, though.*

And then I burst into tears.

Oh, God. Now Josh is actually going to think I'm a basket case. But a friend checked up on me after hearing I was sick. A man fed me noodles and chocolate and made me a hot water bottle. I'm not used to these things, and they're making me all weepy.

"What's wrong?" he asks. "Did you get bad news?"

"No, just someone checking up on me, and I'm weirdly emotional today." I try to smile through the tears. "See? I'm fine."

"Alright," he says uncertainly.

I have a feeling he'd want to beat up anyone who made me cry, which is touching and rather scary.

Once we've finished our soup and dumplings, I pull out the chocolate hazelnut tarts I made yesterday. "A slight modification of my previous recipe," I say. "Tell me what you think."

He moans after his first bite, and I feel the stirrings of lust in my belly, which, for obvious reasons, I didn't feel earlier today, despite his company.

"They're perfect," he says.

I grin. "So here's what I changed…"

I proceed to tell him all about the tarts. I basically recite my recipe, then realize it probably isn't interesting to anyone but me. All that matters to Josh is that they taste good.

"I'm sorry," I say, even though he told me not to say that. "I must be boring you."

"No." He slides his hand through my hair, which I'm sure must be an absolute mess. "You light up when you talk about your work. It's nice."

This time, I don't have to force my smile.

After dinner, he insists on cleaning up. While he does that, I make a horrifying discovery.

I'm out of pads.

I remember thinking to myself at work that I should stop at the pharmacy on the way home, but then Josh came by and we took a cab.

Just as I'm closing my night-table drawer, something starts clawing at my uterus again, and I curl up on my bed. It feels like a baby dinosaur is trying to get out of an egg, and I'm the fucking egg.

Does that comparison make sense? Ugh. I don't know anymore.

I stumble to the kitchen. "Josh, I have a huge favor to ask."

"What is it?"

He throws the dish towel over his shoulder, and damn, that's pretty hot. I almost ask him to do it again, but then I remember my important mission.

"I need you to, uh, get something from the pharmacy for me," I say. "It's just a block away, and this is what you need to buy." I pull out my phone, find a photo of the package of sanitary napkins I require, and hold it up for him to see. "These exact ones. This brand, with wings. They always have them in stock. Nothing different, okay?"

Josh doesn't blink. "No problem. Is that all?"

I nod. "Here, I'll get you some cash."

He holds up a hand. "Don't worry about it."

He makes me another hot water bottle and a cup of tea—which I'm determined to actually drink this time—then heads to the pharmacy. After I take an ibuprofen, I turn on the TV and start an episode of *Brooklyn 99*. Despite the on-and-off pain I'm experiencing, I smile. I feel...cherished.

Josh returns with the pads and some more chocolate, and I nearly declare my love for him again but manage to hold back. We watch a few episodes of the show together, him sitting up on the couch and me lying down with my head in his lap.

By nine thirty, I'm pretty tired.

"You can leave now," I tell Josh. "I'm going to bed. Thank you so much for everything."

"I'll stay, if you don't mind. I can sleep out here on the couch, or—"

"Of course you can stay in the bed."

He smiles at me.

I brush my teeth, put on my pajama shirt, and climb into bed. Josh climbs in with me, wearing his Henley and boxers, and I snuggle up against his chest. I kiss him, trying to express, without words, how much I appreciate all this. When I scrape my fingers over his abs, he hisses out a breath.

"Sarah," he groans.

We leisurely kiss for a while, and then I fall asleep.

I wake up when my alarm goes off the next morning. The large lump in bed next to me slowly begins to move, letting out a few curse words.

"What time is it?" Josh grumbles, rubbing his eyes.

"Five thirty."

"How are you feeling?" He puts his hands on my cheeks, his attention now all on me.

"My uterus is no longer trying to kill me, so I'm much better."

"Are you going to work?"

"Yep."

"Please go home if it gets as bad as yesterday."

I nod.

"Call me if you need to."

"Okay."

"You promise?"

"Yes, I'll call you. Quit bossing me around, Sir CEO. And I must apologize, I don't have the Lucky Charms that you favor for breakfast."

"Then I guess I'll be without my magic powers today."

We look at each other and laugh.

After we drink coffee and eat cereal without mini-marshmallows, I take his head in my hands. "Thank you," I say. "Thank you."

~

I'm in the kitchen at Happy As Pie by six thirty, as usual. Josh went home to shower and change before going into the office, but he's lingering in my thoughts.

Today I'm making lemon meringue, plus banana cream pies with extra cream. Someone called a few days ago, asking for four of the "premier special" pies. They're having a party—I'm not sure what for—and thought it would be funny to serve the pie that was thrown in the premier's face.

I take the pie crusts out of the freezer and put them in the oven.

However, I soon realize I've made a horrible mistake.

When you bake pie crusts blind, without filling, you put weights on top so it doesn't puff up and bake unevenly.

But I forgot to do that.

I hurry to the oven and pull out all of the pie crusts, then put the weights in, like I should have done the first time.

The crusts will be fine, but I'm unsettled by my mistake. I don't make mistakes like this. It's not like me. And it's not the first error I've made this week.

Josh continues to haunt my thoughts for the rest of the morning. Whenever I catch myself smiling for no reason, I knock the smile off my face and force myself to focus on the task at hand.

It's almost noon when my phone rings, and I reach for it with a little too much enthusiasm, thinking maybe it's him. My face falls when I see it's my mother.

"Hi, Mom," I say, walking into my office.

"Hi, sweetie. Guess what?"

"Mr. Albert's sheep escaped again?"

She chuckles, and the familiarity of it makes me smile and tense at the same time.

Parents are complicated.

I haven't seen my mother since Christmas, and I miss her, but at the same time, being around her is such an ordeal.

"We're coming to Toronto on Sunday!" she says. "Me, Megan, and the kids. It's March Break, so Benjy and Rosie are off school. We're going to stay for two nights—we found this cute bed and breakfast on the same street as your pie shop—"

"Kwanzan Cherry Bed and Breakfast?" It's named after the cluster of Kwanzan cherry trees out front, which have gorgeous blossoms in May.

"Yes! That's the one."

I shouldn't be disappointed. I shouldn't.

It's just…

Well, I'd been hoping to spend Sunday night and part of Monday with Josh, and now I'll have to spend time with my family instead.

"That sounds awesome," I say.

"What's wrong, Sarah?"

Ugh, I hate that my mom can read me so well, even over the phone.

"Nothing," I say. "It'll be great to see you!"

"Something's wrong."

"I have cramps, that's all. It's the second day of my period."

Sometimes, I feel like I can't tell my mother anything, and yet I can tell her certain personal things that are hard to talk to anyone else about. Because she's my mother.

Though I don't actually have cramps right now. I had a little pain earlier, but I took some ibuprofen and it did the trick.

My answer seems to satisfy her, though.

"How's business going?" she asks.

"We're going to start catering!" I say brightly. "We're doing a Pi Day party next week."

"Pi Day? What's that?"

"March fourteenth. You know, the third month, fourteenth day…three-point-one-four."

"Right. I see." Though it sounds like my mother doesn't see and is confused by the idea. "All this fancy city stuff that I know nothing about. Are you sure you're ready to do catering, darling? How many pies are you making?"

"A hundred and twenty savory pies and thirty dessert pies."

"A hundred and fifty pies?"

"Plus tarts and salad. Oh, and shortbread cookies."

There's silence on the other end of the phone. My mother seems skeptical that I can pull this off, and I clench the phone too tightly in my hand.

I can do it, dammit. I know I can. I'm good at what I do.

Sure, I screwed up the pie crusts this morning, and I still have a bandage on my finger, and I had to go home early from work yesterday, and…

I will do this, no matter what. It's not too much for me to manage.

Which reminds me… I should go over the schedule for all the work we have to do, since Pi Day is quickly approaching.

"I have to go, Mom," I say.

Naturally, she takes this as an invitation to tell me all the Ingleford gossip that I really don't care about, as well as the articles Aunt Gabby forwarded her yesterday: "Fourteen Unusual Dog Names" and "Nineteen Adorable Names for Your Pet Rock."

Just what I needed, of course.

A few minutes later, I'm reviewing the schedule for next week when Ann pops her head into my office. "Delivery for you."

"Delivery?" I say. "I'm not expecting anything."

I go out front and see a glass vase of yellow roses and baby's breath. Tied to the vase is a small card that says: *Hope you're feeling better. Can't wait to see you tonight. xo Josh*

I grin.

A guy has never sent me flowers before. I never thought I cared much about receiving flowers, but they're so pretty and I love them.

"They're from your CEO boyfriend, I take it," Ann says, waggling her eyebrows.

Somehow, the fact that he sent me flowers makes it more real. It feels like evidence that what happened yesterday—him bringing me home and taking such good care of me when I had cramps—wasn't just a dream.

I'm overwhelmed. I have to cater the perfect Pi Day party next week, and my family is coming to visit me on Sunday. And after a decade of refusing to get close to any man, I now have Josh Yu. Yes, he makes me feel amazing, but if you let someone become an important part of your life, if you let them in past your defenses, they have more power to hurt you.

Although I can't wait to see him again, I need a night to myself. A night to get my head back on straight.

I call Josh to thank him for the flowers and say that I'll need a rain check on dinner tonight. He suggests tomorrow, and I agree. Something more casual than last time, he says.

I stay at work late, going over the financial stuff I didn't get to yesterday.

When I walk home, it's dark, and I hold the vase of roses tightly in my hands, like it's the most important thing in the world, and I keep sniffing them, just because I can.

[19]

JOSH

SARAH HAS a sip of my yuen yeung.

"What do you think?" I ask.

"I prefer my coffee and tea separately, but it's not as weird as I expected."

It's Friday after work, and I've taken her to a cha chaan teng near Happy As Pie. A cheap Hong Kong-style café with an eclectic menu, including lots of Chinese-style Western food and drinks like yuen yeung, a mixture of coffee and milk tea.

Sarah returns to her plain milk tea, no coffee added. She rescheduled our dinner from yesterday to today, saying she was busy at work, and I admit I was disappointed, but I understand. I know what it's like; I work hard, too, and she probably had to make up for the all the things she'd planned to get done on Wednesday.

When I showed up at Happy As Pie two days ago and saw her curled up in a chair, looking like she was ready to pass out or maybe hurl, something twisted painfully in my gut. I hated to see her in pain, and I was overcome with the urge to look after her.

Now, however, she doesn't look sick at all. She's pretty freaking hot in a blue sweater with tempting little buttons.

There's something tentative about her, though. I don't know how else to explain it. She seems more uncertain than usual.

But she's delighted with all the interesting things on the menu, and it takes her a while to decide what to get. She considers trying the borscht, curious how it would be different from the borscht she's had at Eastern European restaurants, but finally decides on black pepper beef with spaghetti, at my recommendation. I get Hainanese chicken. We also share Hong-Kong style French toast, which is basically a peanut butter sandwich on thick slices of white bread that's dipped in egg and milk, then fried. It's served with a pat of butter and drizzled with condensed milk.

"Sometimes jam is used instead," I tell Sarah as she pops another bite in her mouth. I don't try it yet; I just enjoy watching her eat, and it thrills me when she moans in contentment.

"This is what I love about Toronto," she says. "Lots of different food from all over the world. In Ingleford, there's a diner and a Tim Hortons, and that's it. The diner is pretty good, don't get me wrong, but there's so little variety, and as someone who's always loved food, well…"

"When did you move here?"

"When I was eighteen, to study baking and pastry arts. My parents had taken us to Toronto a couple times when we were kids, to see a baseball game and go up the CN Tower. And I loved it. From the time I was ten, I planned to move here when I grew up."

One thing I really like about Sarah: she knows what she wants, and she works to get it. She's driven, and she's amazing at what she does. I have no doubt that everyone at the Pi Day party, including my parents, will think the food is fantastic.

There's a little butter at the corner of her mouth, and I lean forward to wipe it off, then smile at her, our faces close together. My heart is pounding in my chest; being close to her is always thrilling.

Before I can do something inappropriate, I sit back in my chair and have a sip of my yuen yeung.

"So why pie?" I ask.

She shrugs. "I always loved pie, and it puts a smile on people's faces."

I always want to put a smile on her face, too.

There are lots of other restaurants I could take her to, places where she's probably never eaten. She liked the soup from the Shaanxi restaurant—there's a place in Scarborough with that kind of food. The cumin lamb and skewers are amazing. I think she'd enjoy it.

I keep inserting her into my plans for the future. I'm not thinking far in advance, just a nice Sunday dinner maybe a few weeks from now, but for me, that's something. Women have never been part of my plans like that.

Not until Sarah.

It's a little scary, I'm not going to lie. But with her, it seems natural.

It seemed natural to go to the florist and order roses for her, grinning as I imagined her face when she received them.

It seemed natural to go to a jewelry store to buy her a present.

After dinner, we go back to her apartment, planning to watch a movie. Before we cozy up on the couch, I hand her the small package that I've been keeping inside my jacket all evening.

She tears open the paper, revealing a velvet box. It isn't the same size as an engagement ring box—I made sure of it.

She doesn't open it. "Josh, it's too much."

"You haven't seen what's inside."

She bites her lip.

"What's wrong?" I lead her to the couch and take her hands in mine.

"You got me jewelry." That uncertainty is back in her expression

"Nothing fancy. I promise."

I take the box from her and open it up. She laughs when she sees what's inside.

It's a pi necklace: a silver chain with a π pendant.

"Can I put it on for you?"

When she nods, I place the necklace around her neck and do up the clasp.

I like seeing her wear something I bought. I was delighted when I found this.

She fingers the pendant. "I can't afford to be distracted right now. I'm building up my business, making sure it's a success. It's what I've wanted my whole life, and I won't screw it up because of a guy. I really like you, I just…"

"You're not going to be distracted."

"I already am! I sliced my finger open the other day, and that's something I never do."

"Were you thinking about my sexy arm? The one you stabbed with a fork last week?"

She's laughing now, but her expression is still guarded.

I lace my fingers with hers. "I understand that you're committed to your job and making your business succeed—I know what that's like. For a few years, Amrita and I worked *all* the time. I wanted to prove to my dad that I wasn't a failure; she had an awkward relationship with her parents after she came out, and she had something to prove, too. I know you have to work hard, and I respect that, but breaks are healthy, too."

She hesitates. "Josh, you haven't been seeing any other women lately, have you?"

"God, no." I hadn't been interested in a woman for a while before I met Sarah, and since then, there's no way I could have thought of anyone else.

"Didn't think so. Just wanted to be sure." She pauses. "Are we in a relationship?"

"I think so, not that I have much experience."

"Neither do I. I'm used to being alone. Self-contained. I'm not used to feeling vulnerable. But…" She cups my face in her hands.

I capture her mouth with mine, and with my kiss, I try to tell her everything that's hard to put into words. That I see her, that I understand who she is, and that I don't want to change her.

I just want to be with her.

A chopstick hits me in the arm.

"Ow!" I glare at Amrita. She, Eduardo, and I are out for lunch on Saturday after a long morning at the office.

"You're oblivious to the world around you," Amrita says, "and you really should be paying attention. After all, the last time you went out for ramen, you ended up with a…" She smirks.

"Dick burn," Eduardo finishes.

This draws the attention of the family next to us. The mother glowers at Eduardo.

"Which is why we're at this ramen restaurant," I say, "not the one where the, uh, injury occurred."

That's just an extra precaution, though. The chance of a repeat is negligible, but I have bad memories of that restaurant, so I'm not going there again. Especially since another penis injury would be particularly inconvenient right now, seeing as I'm having sex on a regular basis.

I think of Sarah slipping her hand inside my pants, taking my cock in hand…

Focus, Josh. You're at a restaurant.

"You're thinking about Sarah, aren't you?" Amrita says.

I shrug.

"I'm going to tease you mercilessly."

"I can't wait," I deadpan.

"I owe you. You teased me all the time after I met Holly."

"True. I suppose I deserve it."

"I can't wait to meet her at the party on Thursday," Eduardo says. "Shall I tell her about the little ramen incident last year?"

"Too late," I say. "Amrita already relayed that fun tidbit."

He slaps the table and laughs.

Just then, the server comes over with a tray of ramen. She deposits one bowl in front of me without any accidents, but I'm still holding my breath. There are two more bowls of piping-hot broth and noodles to be served.

Fortunately, my friends' bowls also make it onto the table, rather than my lap.

I'm swirling my soup spoon in the broth when my phone buzzes.

TONIGHT. YOU. ME. LOTS OF CHICKS. CLUB PHOENIX.

I put down the phone and massage my temples. I don't know why Neil likes to text in all caps. It gives me a headache.

"Judging by your expression," Amrita says, "I'm guessing it's not Sarah."

"No, it's Neil."

She rolls her eyes.

"Who's Neil?" Eduardo asks.

"Neil Donovan."

"You're friends with Neil Donovan? I didn't think you would be, considering he beat you on the list of most eligible bachelors in Toronto."

"Ha," I say. "Like I care about that."

"Neil's an asshole," Amrita says.

"Nah, I wouldn't go that far. He's just a bit...much."

And right now, I'm not in the mood for Neil's brand of fun, which often involves exclusive clubs with pounding music and writhing bodies. That's his scene, every weekend. Me, I enjoy it every now and then.

At least I did.

But tonight, I have plans to go to Sarah's and eat leftover pie, and that sounds pretty damn spectacular.

I look up at Amrita, who's now doing something horrifying.

She's typing on my phone.

"Give that back." I try to grab it out of her hands, but Eduardo fends off my attack. "What are you telling him?"

She returns my phone a moment later, and I read the message she sent Neil.

Sorry, dude, I met this chick and she's totally rad. I think I'm in love [heart emoji]

"Um," I say. "That doesn't sound like me at all."

A minute later, I get another text.

WHO STOLE YOUR PHONE? Neil asks.

I chuckle. *Amrita.*

TELL HER I SAY HI. AND YOU'RE COMING TONIGHT, RIGHT?

Actually, I did meet a girl...

Neil sends me a whole bunch of emojis that I think are meant to express his general frustration with me as a person.

See, Neil doesn't believe in relationships.

I wouldn't quite say that was me before I met Sarah. It's not that I didn't believe in relationships, but that I chose to focus my time on other things, and I'd never felt as drawn to anyone as I do to Sarah.

Plus, as I realized last week, I felt like I didn't deserve it.

My past still haunts me, but after this party on Thursday, after my dad finally comes to Toronto to see the life I've built here, I hope that will change. And maybe after Sarah caters a kick-ass Pi Day party—I have no doubt she'll succeed—she'll be less worried about a relationship getting in the way of her business.

Yes, Pi Day will be an important day. A silly holiday, but it's taken on such significance in my life.

I start eating my ramen and ignore Neil's further texts. Amrita, Eduardo, and I return to talking about work stuff, rather than my love life—thank God—but Sarah is never far from my mind. I picture her in the kitchen, where she's at ease, wearing an apron and the necklace I gave her yesterday, and...

What if that were all she was wearing?

Now that's a nice thought.

"Earth to Josh!" Amrita says, throwing another chopstick at me.

WHEN MY FAMILY arrives at Happy As Pie on Sunday afternoon, I'm not in a great mood. I've spent an hour trying to fix one of our ovens without success. Of course it had to break right before our busiest week of the year. I'll have to call my repair person and get her to come ASAP.

But when my six-year-old niece rushes toward me, I can't help but smile.

"Auntie Sarah! Auntie Sarah!" Rosie throws her arms around my leg.

"Hi, Rosie," I bend down and give her a hug.

"Mommy says you own a shop that only sells pie. Is that true?"

My niece and nephew have never been to Happy As Pie before. I gesture to the pies in the glass counter. "See, all pie!"

Rosie turns back to her mother, my sister Megan. "It's like heaven!"

"It's her new phrase," Megan says. "Yesterday she said chicken nuggets were like heaven. The day before, she said the same thing about Tim Hortons." She gives me a more restrained hug. "It's great to see you, Sarah. You look good."

Megan and I are close in age—she's only a year and a half

older than me—but our lives are completely different. She went to college in London (London, Ontario, of course) to become a dental hygienist and married her college sweetheart. She now works for the dentist in Ingleford, after taking a few years off when the kids were smaller.

"Where's Mom?" I ask.

Just as the words leave my mouth, my mother walks in.

I immediately go over and give her a hug. It's instinctive. I love my mother, and it's been a while. Still, those words run through my head.

You'll never make it.

But here I am, in my own pie shop, and I'm doing okay, though the cost of the oven repairs weighs heavily on my mind.

"Mommy said we can have two slices of pie each," Rosie says.

"No, I most certainly did not." Megan puts her hands on her hips. "Don't you try to pull that one on me, Rosie."

Benjy tugs on my apron. "Two slices of pie. Please?"

He knows I'm the weakest link. I don't see my niece and nephew often, and yeah, I'm likely to spoil them when I do.

I describe each of the pies. Rosie and Benjy seem confused by the idea of savory pies, but they are very excited by all of the dessert pies. Rosie eventually decides on berry crumble pie, and Benjy chooses banana cream. Megan gets pumpkin pie and lets her children have a tiny taste of it. My mother initially says she's not hungry, but when Megan tells her that's unacceptable, she chooses the lemon-lime tart. She badgers me about my diet, saying I shouldn't eat pie all the time, and about my love life.

"You're thirty-one," Mom says. "Megan had already been married for eight years and had two kids at that age, yet you're still single."

I open my mouth to say, *Actually, I'm seeing someone,* then think better of it.

Megan, however, notices my hesitation and raises her

eyebrows. I suspect she's going to say something when Mom isn't around.

Sure enough, she brings it up the next day. The two of us are getting pedicures while Mom takes the kids to the museum to see the dinosaurs.

It takes a while for us to get to the topic, though. First, Megan tells me about Benjy's birthday party, for which Grandma made a chocolate money cake.

"Remember when you swallowed a dime?" Megan asks.

"How could I forget? I thought I was going to die. Longest two days of my life."

We laugh.

"Well, Dad told Benjy about that," Megan continues. "He said a money tree grew in your stomach, and Benjy wanted to swallow the coins so he could grow his own tree."

"Oh, dear." It's exactly the sort of thing my dad would do. He was always trying to convince us to believe ridiculous things when we were kids. He claimed chocolate milk came from brown cows—which I believed until I was six. "So Benjy decided to swallow the coins on purpose?"

"Fortunately, I heard Benjy bragging to Rosie about how he was going to grow a tree of quarters in his stomach and buy all the candy he wanted. So I put a stop to any deliberate coin-swallowing. Those cakes are hazardous, but Grandma insists on making them."

"A man wanted me to bake an engagement ring into a pumpkin pie," I say. "It was a really nice diamond ring, and I refused. Can you imagine swallowing an engagement ring?"

"And growing a tree of diamond rings in your stomach? Think of how rich you'd be! You might even be able to buy a house in Toronto."

I've missed this. I should do a better job of keeping in touch with my sister. I don't make it down to Ingleford very often, but we have fun together when I do. I've always been closer to her than to my brothers.

"Speaking of diamond rings…" Megan says.

I groan.

"You knew it was coming," she says. "You're seeing someone? How serious is it?"

"I just met him a few weeks ago."

"Details! Come on, this is huge. You haven't dated much in Toronto, although I'm sure there's no shortage of men."

"His name is Josh, and he runs a tech company."

I'm not sure what else to add. He bought me flowers and a pi necklace? I accidentally stabbed him with a fork, and somehow that led to a kiss? I'm catering a Pi Day party for him?

In the end, I say, "He makes me do stupid things because I'm always thinking about him. Today I almost used salt instead of sugar in the shortbread cookies."

I don't usually go into Happy As Pie on Mondays, but I went this morning because we've got a big week ahead of us. I wanted to get the number-shaped shortbread cookies—for a hundred digits of pi—out of the way, since those can be made a few days in advance, and I also needed to be there when the oven repair person arrived.

I cringe when I think of the bill.

And the fact that I nearly ruined all those cookies.

"You, mooning over a guy." Megan chuckles. "I did think you seemed a little different yesterday. In a good way."

"I'm worried," I admit. "I can't afford to keep making errors at work. Is falling in love always like this?"

Although I'm thirty-one, I'm rather inexperienced in this area. Megan, however, is married, and she had a number of boyfriends before that.

"Yeah," she says. "For me, anyway. Just at the beginning, though."

Okay, that makes me feel better.

"Show me a picture of him. Surely you have one on your phone."

While our toenails are being painted, I pull up a photo. Megan looks at it a beat too long before smiling and saying, "He's cute."

I know the reason for her hesitation.

Josh isn't white, and my sister, who lives in a town that's ninety-nine percent white, wasn't expecting that.

A few years ago, the ice cream parlor in Ingleford got a mural painted on the side wall. It shows a diverse group of people enjoying their ice cream cones, something I find pathetically hilarious. There are more visible minorities in that mural than there are in the town, which has one black couple and one Asian family.

Toronto, on the other hand, is very diverse, and I love that. But Megan isn't used to it. I doubt she has a problem with Josh being Asian, but it's a surprise to her.

"Ooh!" Megan says. "He should come to dinner tonight."

"Um." I'm a little uncomfortable with Josh having a family dinner with us. It's pretty early in our relationship for that, isn't it?

But perhaps I could introduce him to my sister. Megan and I are going to the Eaton Centre after this, and his office is only a ten-minute walk from there. We could pop in and say hi.

I'm excited at the thought of seeing him again. I haven't seen him since yesterday morning, which really isn't that long, but I miss him.

This falling-in-love-business is strange.

And it still scares me. I've spent my adult life refusing to develop relationships that might in any way affect my goals. Josh understands my dedication to my job, and he treats me well, and Megan seems to think my silly errors at work will stop soon, but still.

I absolutely cannot fail. I imagine returning to my hometown, tail between my legs, the silly girl who dreamed too big and couldn't make it in the city, and I can't bear the thought. Life in Ingleford is claustrophobic. For some people, it's what they want, and that's great. But it's not for me. It never will be.

I want to live in a city with multiple sushi restaurants within a five-minute walk of my apartment. I want to live in a city where my little pie shop is on the same street as an Indonesian restaurant, an El Salvadoran restaurant, and an Asian-inspired ice cream shop. I like the community feeling of Baldwin Village, but I also like being anonymous when I walk down a major street; nobody knows who I am and who my parents are. And English isn't the only language I hear.

Of course I don't think everyone in Ingleford is an unsophisticated simpleton, but the town *is* rather insular.

"Sarah?" Megan says. "Can I meet him? Please?"

I blow out a breath. I'm catastrophizing. Happy As Pie, despite the recent oven failure, is doing okay. We'll do a great job with this party. We'll get more catering jobs, and I'll build the business I want.

But I can't completely shake my unease.

I must absolutely make sure that Josh doesn't distract me, but despite my niggling uncertainties about our relationship, I'm determined to show my sister—and my mother—that he's a great guy.

So I text him and ask if we can pop into his office.

Josh says he has a meeting soon, but he'll be done in an hour, so any time after that would be good.

After our pedicures, Megan and I head to the Eaton Centre for some shopping, and then we meet my mom and the kids at Dundas Square.

"Sarah has a boyfriend!" Megan squeals. "We're going to see him now!"

Mom raises her eyebrows.

I take out my phone and show her the list of eligible bachelors under thirty-five, hoping she'll be a little impressed that Josh is on it. As with Megan, there's a bit of a hesitation when Mom sees his picture, but then she smiles and says, "He's a CEO? You know, I just read a very good book about a CEO who has quintuplets."

"The CEO's Quintuplet Surprise?" I ask.

"You've read it?"

"Um, no. I was too horrified by the quintuplet part."

We head toward Josh's office. I've never actually been here before, so I'm curious, too. And freaked out and excited for my family to meet him.

"How should I greet him?" Mom asks. "In his culture—"

"Maybe try 'hello'? That always works."

"Why are you being smart with me, Sarah? I just want to make a good impression."

"Treat him like you'd treat any other boyfriend of mine."

"But you haven't had any boyfriends, not since high school. Unless you were hiding them from me?" She looks at me questioningly.

I shake my head. "Josh grew up in Canada. Don't compliment his English, and don't tell him that you like the chicken balls at the Chinese restaurant in the next town over, or that you saw a Bruce Lee movie once."

I don't think my mom will be an awful caricature, but I'm a little worried now.

Crap. Maybe this is a terrible idea.

We arrive at Hazelnut Tech, which is on the second and third floors of a retrofitted old brick building. The space feels modern, yet comfortable and relaxed, and I can totally see this as Josh's workplace.

His assistant, Clarissa, is expecting us, and she shows us into his office.

Josh stands up to greet us and gives my mother and sister one of his dazzling smiles. Seriously, his smile lights me up every time I see him. My mother is clearly charmed as well, and I can't say I'm surprised.

"Aren't you a little young to be a CEO?" she asks.

"I'm a year younger than Mark Zuckerberg, and my company is nowhere near as big as his. Clearly I have some catching up to do."

Mom laughs.

"Are you Auntie Sarah's boyfriend?" Rosie asks.

"Yes," he says.

"Are you going to get married? Can I be the flower girl?"

I can't help tensing up. I'm just getting used to the idea of having a boyfriend, never mind getting married one day.

"We'll see," he says, smiling at Rosie as though he's not bothered by her question, but perhaps he is and just isn't showing it.

"Sarah," Mom says, "there's a new wedding dress maker in London who—"

"Mom!"

At least she didn't say anything about quintuplets. I'd much rather she talk about wedding dresses than five babies. I recall the pain my cramps caused me last week and imagine five babies-to-be in my uterus instead.

Dear God.

"What's with the funny expression?" Megan asks me.

"Uh, Josh and I haven't been together very long, and I think the talk of weddings is a little premature, that's all."

"It's never too early if it's the right guy," Mom says, but fortunately she moves on to another topic. "What does your company do, Josh?"

"Custom software and mobile app development."

"What's an app?"

"You know on your phone—"

"Mom doesn't have a smartphone," Megan cuts in.

"Oh, dear," Mom says. "This all sounds a bit modern for me."

Josh takes out his phone and pulls up the food delivery app he used the other day. With a few clicks, he orders a Hawaiian pizza to the office.

"You don't have to talk to anyone?" Mom asks, perplexed.

"Nope," he says.

"But how does that work?"

"Mom!" Megan says in exasperation. "It's the twenty-first century. Get with the program. Although I think pineapple on pizza is an abomination."

"No," Mom says, "it's delicious. My favorite." She beams at Josh.

We don't wait around for the pizza, though. I hustle my family out after ten minutes so Josh can get back to work and so I don't need to hear any talk about weddings. But I feel proud that this wonderful man has chosen *me*. Though at the same time, I'm disturbed that I brought my family to meet him. I can't believe I did that.

Outside on the sidewalk, the kids are getting antsy.

"Benjy hit me!" Rosie says.

"Did not."

"Did too!"

"That's enough," Megan says. "Let's get some food. What do you want to eat? It's Toronto. You can get anything here."

"Peanut butter sandwich," Rosie says.

"Me, too!" Benjy jumps up and down.

Megan sighs.

"You know," I say, "how would you like peanut butter sandwich French toast?"

And that's how I end up at a cha chaan teng for the second time in a week.

While we're eating our Hong Kong-style French toast and Macau-style Portuguese chicken, someone in an inflatable T-Rex costume walks by the window, and the kids screech with delight.

I love Toronto.

IT'S PI DAY.

I didn't go into the office this morning. Instead, I did some work at home, and now I'm driving to a restaurant in North York to meet my parents for dim sum, which was my mom's idea. Toronto has a much larger Chinese community than Ottawa, and there are way more food options. She told me to pick a restaurant, and I picked a fairly fancy one, as far as dim sum places in Toronto go.

I can't help freaking out, which is rare. I run a business; I'm used to important meetings.

But my father is in a class of his own.

My dad is a big, balding man with a salt-and-pepper beard, which he keeps neatly trimmed. He's been going gray since I was a kid, but it's as though, through sheer willpower, he has prevented himself from going completely gray. He looks a little like the father in *Kim's Convenience*, and weirdly, I've started watching that show because I miss my dad.

But today, I hope he'll actually speak to me.

My father can be stern and demanding and even ruthless, but

he's devoted to my mother, and he loves my sisters and his grandchildren, who delight in getting him to play horsey.

When I was little, I wanted to make him proud, and when I was a bit older, I wanted to piss him off—which I did.

Now I want him to be proud of me again. I want him to acknowledge I'm his son and actually wish me a merry Christmas when I go to Ottawa in December. That's what I've wanted more than anything for years.

I want my father back.

I get to the restaurant twenty minutes early, as there's no way I'm going to be late, but there's another reason, too.

I want to slip the server my credit card before my parents arrive.

In many Asian families, people fight over the bill. Not that I've actually eaten at a restaurant with my father in my adult life, but I know he'll try to pay the bill, and I'm determined to pay it myself.

Fighting over the bill can actually get rather vicious and lead people to do ridiculous things. I remember going out for dinner with my aunt's family, the only extended family we have in Canada. My father snuck the waitress his credit card after ordering, and my aunt was pissed when the end of the meal came and she discovered the bill had already been paid. She chased my dad through the restaurant with a wad of cash in her hand. When he ran outside and opened the car door, she threw the money on the driver's seat before he could stop her, then used an umbrella to fend him off when he tried to return the money.

With that memory in mind, I open the door to the restaurant and immediately see my parents seated at a table near the back. Guess I won't be able to covertly hand over my credit card before the meal. I'll need to make other plans.

But for now, I won't focus on the bill.

My pulse hammers as I approach the table. "Hi, Mom."

She stands up to greet me with a hug.

Dad, on the other hand, merely grunts.

Oh, is this how it's going to be? The three of us having dim sum, and he *still* isn't going to talk to me?

But then he nods and says, "Josh."

The first word he's said to me in ages. My name.

"Hi, Dad." I attempt a smile as I sit down.

Meeting Sarah's family on Monday was a cakewalk compared to this. I'm afraid that if I say the wrong word, Dad will go back to the silent treatment.

"How was the drive?" I ask. "You must have left quite early this morning."

Dad grunts again. "Lots of construction."

I'm hanging on every meaningless word, because it doesn't feel meaningless, not to me. He's actually answering my questions.

I hold up the order sheet, where we write down how many of each dish we want. "Do you want to order, or should I?"

He clucks his tongue. "If you do it, there will be siu mai and bao and nothing else. Better let me."

I laugh. He remembers exactly what I like at dim sum, even though it's been years. Except my tastes are a little more varied now than when I was a child.

Dad orders a generous amount of things, including turnip cakes, which none of us particularly like, but he enjoyed teasing me with them when I was little—I'd always wrinkle my nose.

Is that why he orders them now? I don't know.

The server comes back and takes our order sheet, and when she leaves, Dad looks at me and says, "So, how have you been?"

"In the past seventeen years?" I can't help saying.

He gives me a tight-lipped smile. "Well?"

And so I tell him about my life, though I suspect he already knows all about it—my mother probably tells him everything. He expresses disgust, as expected, at the fact that my business involves making apps for smartphones.

"Ah, so many people, all they do is stare at their phones all day." He shakes his head. "And you make it even worse!" The chicken feet, which are his favorite, arrive as he says this. He tries one and says, "A little too salty."

The little digs and complaints—that's normal. If my father didn't complain at all, that would be a red flag. I'm glad he's acting like himself in front of me. "A little too salty" is high praise from him, so I don't think he's disappointed in my choice of restaurant. If, instead, he said, "It's the most delicious thing I've ever tasted!" I would wonder if he'd started smoking the stuff I used to smoke in high school.

The siu mai and har gow—shrimp dumplings—are next, and we continue to avoid any touching family reconciliation scenes. We don't talk about the Pi Day party at all. There will be time for that later.

However, when I stand up while we're waiting for our egg tarts, my father jerks my arm and pulls me back into my seat.

"Where do you think you're going?" he demands.

"The bathroom."

He gives me a look.

He's not wrong.

I've drunk about fifteen small teacups of tea and I do need to relieve my bladder, but I'd also planned to pay the bill while I was up.

He clucks his tongue again. "That's the oldest trick in the book. I'm disappointed in you. So predictable, not at all sneaky. How are you a good businessman?"

"You don't have to be sneaky to be a good businessman," I say. "What kind of stuff do you think I do?"

"I know what you were doing in high school. Skipping class to smoke marijuana."

"You sound so uncool," Mom says. "Nobody says 'marijuana.' It's 'pot' or 'weed,' isn't that right, Josh? And it's legal now."

"Hold on a second," I say. "Dad, are you suggesting that my company is a front for drug dealing?"

"Ah, silly boy. You know I'm kidding." He's still gripping my arm. "But you are *not* going to the washroom. It's a cheap trick."

"Fine, fine," I grumble. I suppose I can wait.

The egg tarts arrive. I'm stuffed, but that won't stop me from having an egg tart now, or from eating lots of delicious pie later on.

I use a chopstick to draw a pi symbol in the custard filling of one of the tarts. For the pies she's serving tonight, Sarah made steam holes in the shape of the pi symbol, which is a nice touch. Her idea, of course, not mine.

I hand the tart to my dad. "Happy Pi Day."

"I can't believe you're having a Pi Day party," he says. "I thought you were too cool for that, with all your Facebook and Twitter and apps. Though I'm disappointed the party doesn't start at one fifty-nine."

That's the ideal time for a Pi Day party to start, since those are the next three digits of pi after 3.14. But... "I didn't want the party to be in the middle of the workday. And speaking of Facebook, I found your account."

My father's eyes widen in horror, and oh, I'm enjoying this.

"What?" Mom says. "You got Facebook? After you forbid me from getting it?"

"How did you find my account?" Dad asks.

"You friended Nancy," I say. "Did you think she wouldn't tell me?"

Mom turns to me. "What does he do on Facebook? Does he post pictures of us?"

"No, just lame math jokes."

"Wah, they're not lame," he says. "They're brilliant!"

"Well, then, I hope you enjoy the party tonight. I even have math joke napkins."

Dad laughs. It's the first time in forever that he's actually laughed at something I said.

I smile. "He even has a fan club," I tell my mother. "Two

hundred forty-three of his former students are in the Facebook group."

"Two hundred forty-three?" he says. "Last time I checked, there were only two hundred and thirty. How often do you check my fan club?"

Too often, apparently, but my father's unlikely Facebook presence was the closest I could get to him. Until now.

The server comes over with the bill, and the instant she sets it on the table, I grab it.

"I'm paying," I say.

Dad tries to grab it back, but I hold it above my head.

"No, I'm your father," he says. "Your elder. I pay."

"I invited you to this restaurant."

"But going out for dim sum was my idea," Mom interjects. "We pay."

I pull out my wallet and shove a hundred-dollar bill toward the waitress.

She frowns. "What about the card you gave us earlier?" She holds up a payment terminal and a credit card. "Can I put it on this?"

What on earth...

Dad is smirking.

"Did you get here early just so you could give them your credit card?" I ask.

He nods triumphantly. "One hour early."

An hour? But they drove all the way from Ottawa. They must have had to wake up super early, all so they could pull this over me.

"You wouldn't let me go to the washroom," I say. "Why, if you'd already given them your card? And why were you trying to grab the bill back from me?"

"Just messing with you." He crosses his arms over his chest, then enters his pin when the server hands him the machine. "Fun, no?"

I roll my eyes. Alright. Point to my father.

I could try to shove some money in his hand, or steal his car keys and leave the cash on the front seat. But for now, I let him have his victory, because for the first time in twenty years, things aren't terrible between us.

~

After dim sum, my parents want to do a little shopping, so I head back to my house without them. At four o'clock, Amrita and Clarissa come over, and we set up the house for the party. Moving things out of the way as needed, setting up folding chairs and folding tables covered in pi tablecloths. This probably would have worked better as a casual summer party in the backyard, but alas, Pi Day is in March, and there's still snow on the ground.

Sarah arrives with the appetizer tarts, dessert pies, and salads. She's accompanied by her friends, Chloe and Valerie, who will help serve the appetizers. They're all dressed in black pants and white shirts, and when Sarah smiles at me, my heart bounces around in my chest.

"How did dim sum go?" she asks as she arranges the shortbread cookies in order of the digits of pi on a dark wooden serving board.

"Good, I suppose. My dad talked to me, and he got there an hour early to give them his credit card so I couldn't pay."

The other day, I explained to Sarah the antics of my family when it comes to paying the bill, and she looked at me in bafflement.

She laughs now, but then her expression sobers.

I put my hands on her shoulders. "What's wrong?"

She doesn't look at me. "I just really want this to go well. What if Fatima and Dylan screw up the savory pies somehow? What if nobody likes the appetizer quiches and tarts?"

"You've got this. I believe in you." I press a kiss to her temple.

"Everything you make is amazing, and this will be only the start of your catering business, okay?"

She nods. I'm not sure she fully believes me, but I hope she does.

My parents return at five o'clock, after going to multiple Chinese supermarkets to get things they can't buy in Ottawa.

Mom slips off her shoes in the entryway. "This is your house? Wow."

Dad grunts. "You have illegitimate children you didn't tell us about? Is that why you need all this space?"

"It's really not that big," I protest.

"But in Toronto, everything is small. You should save for retirement instead."

"I'm not lacking in money. I can afford what I have. I can afford to throw a Pi Day party for my employees. Here, I'll show you the guest bedroom."

I take my parents upstairs. When they come back down, my dad examines the math joke napkins, which are sitting on one of the tables. He grunts again, but this time, there's some laughter behind the grunt, and I'll take it.

My father is still talking to me and occasionally laughing, and that's more than I've had in a very long time.

By six thirty, the party is in full swing. People are gathered in little groups around my house, some sitting at tables, chatting together. A couple children are running around. I greet everyone who comes in and put their jackets on the extra racks I had Clarissa order for this event. Chloe and Valerie are walking around with platters of quiches and mini tarts. The mushroom and cheese ones are my favorite, but I've restrained myself—I've only eaten two. I haven't seen Sarah in a while, but I know she's in the kitchen, heating up the appetizers and getting the salads ready to serve with dinner. The bartender I hired—Sarah arranged it—is making cocktails and pouring wine, and one of her employees will arrive any minute with the hot savory pies.

I told Sarah earlier that I wouldn't introduce her to my parents tonight, at least not as anything more than the caterer. My dad talked to me for the first time in well over a decade today; I don't want to spring a girlfriend on him, too.

But next time, I'll introduce them.

I don't know when next time will be, but maybe it'll actually be before Christmas.

My father is in the living room, gesturing animatedly with a cocktail as he speaks to a couple of the project managers, who are hanging on his every word. My father can be charming—in a slightly grumpy way, but charming nonetheless—and that's what he's doing tonight. He's probably telling embarrassing stories from my childhood, and I'll hear all about it tomorrow.

I can't wait.

No, really, I can't. This is all going the way I want, and although the party was my idea, I owe its success to Sarah, who helped me plan it and made the delicious food. I peek into the kitchen, and when I see her, I smile and my heart rate kicks up a notch.

She did it.

And she's mine.

JOSH IS GIVING A LITTLE TALK, thanking everyone for coming, saying this year has been great for business so far, and he's looking to hire a few more developers. He's magnetic, and people listen to him when he talks. He doesn't exude power—which is how the heroine describes the hero in *A Secret Baby for the CEO* when she's not calling him an asshole—but he has an air of friendliness and trust, and I can see that everyone here respects him.

Except maybe his father.

His father is magnetic, too, and I can see how he was popular as a teacher, but he has a surliness to him that Josh doesn't.

And I can't forget that he basically disowned Josh.

I also overheard him say that the braised lamb and rosemary pie had too much rosemary, and that annoyed me.

He's wrong. My pie has the perfect amount of rosemary.

Trust me, I spent years getting it just right. His taste buds are broken.

But now the savory pies are finished, and the dessert pies are spread out on the dining room table. There's pumpkin, spiced apple, pear ginger crumble, strawberry-rhubarb, and many others, plus the special pies and tarts I made just for this party, as well as whipped cream and vanilla ice cream. People are taking pictures as they ooh and aah. Hopefully they'll post the photos on Instagram and tell their friends, and I'll get more business. And be known for something other than making the banana cream pie that once adorned the premier's face.

This table is like my life's work. Sure, it's just pie, but pie makes people happy. Sometimes people need something to make them smile, and I can provide that.

And you know what? Josh has always believed in me.

It hits me then.

I've been thinking that my budding relationship with Josh will be to the detriment of my business, just because I made a few silly mistakes in the kitchen. But I'll stop making those mistakes, won't I? What's more important is that Josh makes me feel good and he believes in me. He asked me to do this party, and he knew I'd succeed.

And I did.

His dad's eyes light up when he tries the Nutella pie. A woman moans in bliss after a bite of pear ginger crumble pie.

Since the very beginning, Josh has thought that I'm amazing at what I do, and his belief in me never wavered. I'm not used to having someone in my corner like this.

And having something else to think about, other than my business, is good for me. As I've been told, I might burn out if I think about Happy As Pie all day, every day. It's good for me to have Josh, to have someone to spend time with me. Someone who understands and respects how important my business is to me.

Before, I assumed that any relationship would hurt my dream, but I was wrong. There's no reason for me to avoid relationships, not with someone like Josh.

I catch his eye across the room. When he smiles at me, my

heart flutters in my chest, and I can't help wishing I could steal a kiss.

"Sarah?"

I turn. It's Valerie, and she looks a little pale.

"What's wrong?" I ask.

"Headache."

"You can go home. It's fine. I can handle everything else."

"You sure?"

I nod.

She looks at all the people gathered in Josh's house. "I used to do what they do."

"An ice cream shop sounds more fun than programming."

"Ice cream is Chloe's dream, not mine."

Valerie looks sad, which isn't an emotion I've seen on her face before. She's more likely to be a little prickly and sarcastic.

"Why did you quit?" I ask.

She shrugs. "Because men are assholes."

"Josh said he's looking to hire some people. You could apply? I'm sure he wouldn't let his employees act like assholes."

"No, I think that part of my life is finished."

"Don't say that!" I'm in a good mood. I believe everyone's dreams can come true. After all, I have my own bakery, and we just successfully catered our first party. I have a boyfriend and a couple new friends.

My life is as good as it can be. I need to believe Valerie can have that, too.

After she leaves, I eavesdrop on a bunch of people telling stories about the Pi Day parties at their universities. One man describes how the math department would order a bunch of pizzas and buy a few pies at the grocery store.

Everyone agrees this party is superior.

Of course they do. Not only is my food freaking awesome but there's also alcohol. I'm skeptical that an event hosted by the math department would have alcohol.

It really is the ultimate Pi Day party that Josh desired.

His parents approach me.

"My son says you own the pie shop," his father says.

My son. I bet his dad hasn't said that in a long time. I'm thrilled the party brought the two of them together again, thrilled I could do that for Josh, since I know how much his family means to him.

Though to be honest, it takes some restraint not to tell his dad off for the way he's treated Josh—and for the fact that he thinks my lamb pie has too much rosemary.

"The butter tarts are even better than mine," his mother says.

"I like the hazelnut tarts," his dad says. "Both the maple and the chocolate. Interesting that he named his company Hazelnut Tech. Why name a company after a nut?"

He did it because hazelnuts are your favorite. But I don't say that.

"Well, there's Apple," I say instead. "Not a nut, obviously, but..."

"True. I thought that was a stupid name, too. But the food is delicious."

"Thank you."

A few minutes later, I hear him telling someone that smartphones are stupid, which I'm sure is the appropriate thing to say at a party for a company that does app development.

Josh comes up to me when I'm cleaning up in the kitchen.

"You don't need to do that now," he says. "Enjoy yourself. We can do it together after the party's over."

"There's something else I'd rather do after the party." I wink.

I need to be with him tonight. I need to show him just how much he means to me.

"We have to be quiet," Josh whispers, "since my parents are down the hall."

He presses me back against the door in his bedroom and kisses his way down my neck as he unbuttons my white shirt—which, unfortunately, has a cherry pie stain—and throws it to the floor. He hurriedly strips off the T-shirt I'm wearing underneath, along with my bra, and I can't wait to get him naked, too. I tear off his Henley and push down his jeans.

"Sarah," he gasps as I drop to my knees.

His cock is heavy between his legs, and with a few strokes, he's rock hard, and I take him in my mouth.

I love having my mouth full of him, love the way he's practically tearing out my hair, the desperate, hushed noises he's making. I wrap one hand around the base, and I run my other hand up his strong thighs to his firm abs. His body is a masterpiece, but he's so much more than a warm body in my bed at night.

He's the man who fed me noodles and chocolate, made me a hot water bottle, and went to the store to buy pads for me when I had terrible menstrual cramps.

He's the man who believes in me, and always will.

He helps me relax; he lets me be myself.

Everything is *more* with him.

I give him everything I have. The best fucking blowjob? Yes, I can do it.

Josh probably has no trouble finding women, but he chose *me*. I know I'm special to him. He makes me feel special every day.

I touch the pi pendant around my neck before I squeeze his dick and take him deep in my mouth. My inner muscles clench.

He growls. "I'm going to come if you keep that up."

I release him, just long enough to say, "I want you to come in my mouth." And then I suck him vigorously. He shoves his hands into my hair and tips his head back against the door, eyes shut.

This won't be the only time tonight. I feel insatiable, and I think he does, too. We're both on top of the world; the things we wanted so badly are happening for us. And we need to share it with each other.

He explodes in my mouth. I've never sucked a guy to completion before, but I relish the feel of his cum trickling down my throat. It's crude, a contrast to the feelings I have for him, but with Josh, it feels right.

He slides to the floor and wraps his arms around me.

"We can't have sex in the bed tonight," he says.

"Why not?"

"It squeaks, and we're not alone."

He stands up, tosses a couple pillows from the bed onto the rug, and turns on the lamp on the bedside table.

I feel naughty, and it's delightful.

Once we're lying on the rug, pillows under our heads, Josh begins stroking between my legs, running his fingers over my entrance and playing with my clit. I buck my hips toward him, trying to get more, but he keeps up his slow and steady torture.

On and on he touches me, making me squirm even more. He presses kisses all over my face and neck and breasts, never stopping his ministrations between my legs. When he slides two fingers inside me and curls them upward, I gasp. A few more thrusts, and I'm coming for him.

"I need you," I say.

He rolls on a condom and slides into me as I'm still shuddering.

"Shh," he says. "I've got you."

He makes love to me, utterly filthy and tender all at once. His strokes are slow and deep, and they make me feel things I didn't even know I could feel. I would do anything for him, but I also know he'd never ask me to do something that would hurt my happiness, that would get in the way of my dreams.

He's part of my dreams now, too.

We are joined, so intimately.

I nearly cry out his name when my orgasm overtakes me, but

he covers my mouth with his hand, which somehow is pretty freaking hot. Then he replaces his hand with his mouth and kisses me as he stays motionless inside me. Slowly, he starts to move again, and I grab his ass as he buries himself deep inside me and comes again.

Afterward, he picks me up from the floor and puts me in bed, tucking the pillow under my head. "You were amazing tonight." He strokes my cheek. "The party was amazing."

I knew that, but pride still blooms in my chest at his words.

"I hope you got to eat some of the pie," he says.

"I ate dinner before the party. Don't want to eat while I'm catering."

"You definitely deserve to have some now."

He throws on a robe and heads downstairs. A few minutes later, he returns with a plate of cherry and pumpkin pie, flavors that don't go together at all, but it looks perfect to me right now. He feeds me a piece of pumpkin pie, and I smile as I remember the first time we did this and I managed to stab him with a fork.

Maybe I shouldn't smile at a memory that involved blood, but that's when we had our first kiss and he took off his shirt, so in other ways it's a happy memory.

And now, we're sitting in bed after sex, feeding each other pie, and I'll remember this fondly, too. I have so many lovely memories with Josh, and I haven't known him all that long.

How did I think he would derail my life? The truth is the exact opposite.

He supports me. He helps me reach for what I want.

"I love you," I say.

CAREFULLY, I set down my fork. "You...love me?"

"You don't have to say it back," Sarah says. "I know it's fast, and I can wait for you to feel the same way about me. You care for me, and that's enough."

There's a tremor in her voice. I suspect she's never said these words to a man before, and yet she said them to me.

Actually, she said "I love you" on the night she had terrible cramps and I brought her chocolate, but she didn't mean it the way she means it now.

I'm touched, though I feel uneasy at the same time. I can't help it.

It scares the crap out of me.

Do I love her back? Maybe I do. I'm not sure. I don't really know what love is supposed to feel like, but yes, I do care for her very much, and I want to be with her whenever I can.

All sorts of strange feelings are swirling inside me, but I can't tell Sarah, not now. Not when I'm naked in bed with her, a plate of pie between us.

Instead of speaking, I put the pie on the bedside table, and I pull her into my arms and kiss her. Gently, I stroke my tongue against hers; I show her how I feel rather than tell her, because I can't figure out what to say. I hold her against me from behind, planting kisses on her neck and shoulders, and then I realize she's fallen asleep.

She's been up since five o'clock, baking pies for my party. She's had a long week.

I pull the covers up to her chin, and I stare at her in the faint light of the lamp.

Today was a triumphant day for both of us.

However, it doesn't feel triumphant anymore, not for me. My father actually acknowledged my presence and spoke to me, but it's a bit anti-climactic to have everyday conversation with my dad after so long. Nothing seems meaningful enough.

And nothing changes the fact that he didn't talk to me for almost two decades.

That's my experience of love. My father, who should have loved me no matter what, refused to even say "hello" to me.

Here's the thing. Love is not unconditional, and I will, at some point, screw up, and Sarah won't love me anymore. I can't bear the thought of seeing the disappointment on her face.

I'm not sure I want anything to do with love. It will ultimately lead to pain, and perhaps I had it right when I avoided all relationships for so long.

Except...

Next to me, Sarah is breathing rhythmically in her sleep. She's curled up on her side, her hair going this way and that.

Being with her is pretty wonderful.

I just have trouble believing it can last.

I wake up when my alarm goes off at six. Sarah is already awake, and she's looking at something on her phone.

"Morning," I say, and she turns toward me.

I feel a little better now that I've slept, even if it was a fitful sleep.

A lot better now that I see she's still naked and the blanket is pushed down below her breasts. The tips of her nipples are rosy, and the slopes of her breasts are enticing, and she's got a seductive smile on her lips.

Fuck, I need to be inside her.

I need to push aside the uncomfortable thoughts I had last night; I need to lose myself in her body. Make her mine physically, even if I don't know if it can be anything more.

I need her, and I don't want to be gentle.

I curve my hand over her ass and bring her against me, kissing her desperately. She's as enthusiastic as I am, and when I thrust my fingers inside her, she's already wet, and I growl.

Quietly, of course, so as not to wake my parents.

"I want to be rough," I say. "Is that okay?"

She nods, her lips parted. When her tongue darts out to lick her bottom lip, I nearly lose it. I pull her out of bed and bend her over, her hands gripping the quilt.

Then I roll on a condom and slam into her from behind.

I take her hard, one hand stroking her clit at a punishing pace. She feels amazing. Wet and tight, and she's making these little gasps, just for me. I slow my pace when she shudders around my cock, but a minute later, I'm back to pounding her hard, taking all that I can get. I bite her shoulder and she cries out, muffling herself by pressing her face into the bed. That spurs me on. I grab her beautiful ass and slam into her a few more times before reaching my own release.

Limbs tangled, we collapse on the bed. I adore the feeling of her bare skin on mine. Not just when we have sex, but in the quieter moments afterward. I have her all to myself, this incredible woman who says she loves me. It seems too good to be true.

"I'll leave soon," she says.

No! I don't want her to leave.

"I need to head to the bakery," she continues, "and I'm sure you don't want your parents to see me. Which is fine. I understand. I brought some clean clothes, just in case I ended up staying the night. I'll have a shower, then get going."

I nod.

When she heads to the en suite bathroom, I pad downstairs, thinking I'll make her some coffee before she heads to work. Maybe she'll be interested in some Lucky Charms, too.

But when I reach the kitchen, I can already smell coffee.

My father is sitting at the kitchen table, looking broodingly at a Hazelnut Tech mug.

When he sees me, he gets up to pour another cup of coffee, no milk or sugar. He doesn't know how I like my coffee; he doesn't know so many things about me.

"We need to talk," I say, taking a seat across from him. This is the perfect time. It's just the two of us, and that's how I want to have this conversation.

He surprises me by saying, "I know. We do."

I thought he'd try to avoid a serious conversation.

"You didn't talk to me for seventeen years," I say.

He nods.

"I know I was a difficult teenager. But seventeen years?"

He doesn't look at me. "Your mother didn't need the stress you were causing her."

"I know."

"Our friends were all immigrants, too, with big expectations for their kids."

"And the so-called problems they had to deal with were their children getting a B on a test or deciding to major in English."

He manages a small smile. "Yes. Something like that. And you were throwing away your future. Bringing shame to our family. Being a terrible influence on Melinda, who had always been a good girl."

"I didn't pressure her." I need him to understand that. "And if most of this is about Mom, she didn't need the stress of you refusing to talk to me. Don't you see how messed up this is? I was desperate for your approval, and there was nothing I could do to get it. Nothing."

He sighs and glances down at his coffee, and when he looks up at me, there's an expression on his face that I've never seen before.

"I was wrong," he says.

Did I hear that right? Dad admitting the error of his ways seems as unlikely as him moving to Scotland and buying a Shetland pony farm.

And yet.

I wait for him to continue.

"I was wrong to do what I did, and then I was too proud to admit I'd been wrong." He pauses. "I'm sorry. I shouldn't have gone so long without talking to you. That's on me. It seemed easier to continue that way than to have this conversation." He gestures between us.

I blow out a breath. "So why now? What changed?"

"Your party. I knew it was all for me. The son I knew wouldn't throw a Pi Day party just because."

"To be fair, you don't really know me anymore."

"No, and that's my fault." He has a sip of coffee. "But when your mother told me about the party, and I realized how much effort you were going to...I couldn't say no. I know you think I'm heartless, but—"

"I don't think that."

"So what do you think?"

I don't know how to put it into words, so I say, "You're my father, and nothing can change that, even if you pretended I didn't exist."

"I thought of you every day. I was desperate to hear news about you from your mother and sisters."

"Yet you were too stubborn and proud to pick up the phone and call me yourself."

"Yes. But *you* weren't too proud to have a Pi Day party, with math joke napkins and pi tablecloths."

"It's not as out-of-character for me as you seem to think."

"Perhaps, but I figured if you could set aside your pride, then I could, too. I also knew it would please your mother for us to finally visit you in Toronto."

I pull out a wad of bills from my pocket. "You shouldn't have paid for dim sum."

He shakes his head. "I outsmarted you by getting to the restaurant an hour early. You should accept that."

I chuckle. "You know I have lots of money."

"Yes, look at this house, so unnecessary for one man!"

I could have gotten a swanky condo downtown, but I bought a house instead, and I won't lie: it was partly because I thought a house would impress my parents more, and I didn't think they'd appreciate having to drive to downtown Toronto and park in a garage.

"I named the company Hazelnut Tech because of you. Because you like hazelnuts."

"Such a stupid reason." He's smiling, though.

"Many of the things I did…they were for you. I just wanted you to talk to me again. I wanted to make you proud."

"I am proud." He reaches across the table and taps my wrist, which is a lot of physical affection for him. "Though a company that designs apps for people with those silly smartphones? That's not what I would have chosen."

"I'm still a bit of a rebel. And you'll get a smartphone soon enough, so you can look at Facebook when you're in line at the grocery store."

He looks horrified, and I smile.

We're making progress. My father has said he's proud of me, and that's a lot of what has driven me for the past seventeen years. Making him proud. I never completely gave up on the hope that he'd change his mind, despite all the years of silence, and now, here we are.

I think of Sarah, who told me she loved me. Last night, it seemed impossible that she could stay with me, but now, the impossible seems possible.

"I forgive you," I say to my father.

He nods in acknowledgement, and we sip our coffee in silence for a minute. It's the most comfortable minute I've had with him in a long time.

"Josh, you made coffee?" Sarah walks into the kitchen, wearing jeans and a sweater, her hair slightly damp. "Just what I need."

Dad frowns. "Who's this? Wait, aren't you the caterer?"

Sarah freezes.

Oh, crap.

When I saw my father here, I should have told Sarah. Should have figured out how to sneak her out of the house. But instead, the possibility of having a proper talk with my father made me forget everything else.

Dad stands up, knocking the table in the process, and turns to me, his face red. "I thought you had changed. But no, it's just like before. You have a party, and you sleep with the caterer? While your parents are guests? Tacky."

I cringe. "Dad, Sarah is my girlfriend."

"No, you just say that now to save face!'"

"Josh is telling the truth," Sarah says.

"Then why didn't you introduce her as your girlfriend?" Dad demands. "That's what you would have done if it was the truth."

"You hadn't spoken to me in seventeen years. *Seventeen years.* Introducing you to a girlfriend would have made things complicated. I planned to do it next time."

Except now everything is unraveling in front of my eyes.

"How long have you been together?" Dad asks.

"A couple weeks."

"Even if that's true, she shouldn't have been sleeping over. It's not serious."

"It's serious." I know I sound unsure. My doubts are coming back in full force.

"A few weeks is not serious."

"Josh is an adult," Sarah says to my father. "This is his business, not yours, and he can do what he wants. He treats me well, so you don't have to worry about that."

"I'm an adult, too, and I can decide not to speak to him again! He's thirty-three years old, and he's still making the same mistakes and getting carelessly involved with women."

"Dad! I am not—"

"You are. You were careless with Melinda, and it hasn't changed."

It's all slipping through my fingers. Seventeen years to get to the point where we could have a reasonable conversation, and now it's gone.

God, why did Sarah have to walk in?

"What's going on down here?" My mother enters the room.

"We're leaving," Dad says. "Best to go before rush hour starts."

"What happened?"

"Your son seduced the caterer." He gestures vaguely in Sarah's direction.

"She's my girlfriend," I say.

"You hid the fact that you have a girlfriend from your own mother?" Mom asks.

"Don't listen to him," Dad says. "He's lying that she's his girlfriend."

"For fuck's sake." Sarah steps forward as my parents bristle at the swear word. "He's not lying. I'm his girlfriend, but this makes it all too clear why he didn't want to introduce me to you yesterday."

It's at this point that I notice she's wearing the pi necklace. I remember her reluctance when she saw the jewelry box; I remember her saying that I was a distraction, that I was making her do stupid things like slice her finger open in the kitchen.

And then yesterday, she said, "I love you."

I ball up my fists.

My father takes my mother's hand and walks toward the door, and I don't stop him. I don't see the point.

Thinking I'd actually have my father again? That was too good to be true.

He told me he was proud of me.

And then? He snatched it all away.

The door closes behind them, and I turn to Sarah.

"Your father is a piece of work," she says. "I'm sorry, I didn't realize he was down here with you."

For most of my childhood, there was a picture on the mantle of my dad holding me at the hospital, not even an hour after I was born, looking so happy. My father, who would clean my scraped knees and sing Cantonese lullabies to me.

And then…it was gone.

Eventually, Sarah will get fed up with me, too. Love is conditional, and one day, she'll close the door for the last time.

I blow out a breath. "We need to break up." I'm better off alone. I can see that now.

She cocks her head to the side. "You don't mean that, right?"

"I say what I mean. We need to break up."

"Because your father said you were getting 'carelessly involved with women'? He seems to have puritanical beliefs when it comes to relationships. We've done nothing wrong, and I know you've had a bunch of casual sex in the past, and there's nothing wrong with that, either. I'm sure you never coerced anyone, and I'm sure you were respectful and safe."

"Not with Melinda."

"And I bet that incident made you obsessive about safe sex."

It did. I had sex without a condom once. Only once. And it changed everything. I would never, ever be so stupid again.

I blow out a breath. "Yes, my dad is a bit rigid, but he'd finally apologized to me, and then you came in and—"

"You were silent! I didn't know there was anyone in the kitchen until it was too late. Like I said, I'm sorry. But now you're talking about breaking up? I don't understand."

"You said you love me!" I say accusingly.

"I do."

"Love is temporary. Love is conditional. And I can't go through that again."

"Come on, Josh. I'm not your father. I won't dump you because you make one mistake."

I grasp the pendant around her neck. "When I gave this to you, you told me I was distracting you from work, from your dream. I can't imagine you'll want to keep me around."

She cringes as I throw her words back in her face.

"I was wrong," she says. "You're not a distraction. You're an important part of my life."

I can't accept her words. "You'll change your mind."

"No. Now that I've realized the truth, I won't change my mind. I won't decide that being with you is bad for me."

"It's better to end this now. It'll hurt even more later on."

"Who says it has to end?"

"Because that's just the way it works!" I raise my voice. I can't help it.

"Your parents are still together. My parents are still together."

"That's just the way it works for *me*," I amend.

"You haven't even tried to have a relationship since high school…until now."

"So? Neither have you."

"That's true," she admits, reaching for me. "We can learn how to do this together."

I jerk my hand away from her. "No. I can't. I'll do something foolish, and you'll fall out of love with me, and it'll be just what I deserve."

"Why are you saying it's what you deserve?"

"Even my own father wants nothing to do with me."

"Your father is an ass. I understand why you want his approval, but you have to let go."

"What about you?" I shoot back. "Your mother said you would fail, and it's been gnawing at you ever since. Is that why you're so determined to turn your pie shop into an empire?"

"An empire? I just want a few shops, and to sell pies in some Toronto grocery stores. And that's what *I* want—I'm not doing it just to prove her wrong. Unlike you, who became a goddamn CEO so your dad would be proud of you, and guess what? He still didn't want to talk to you. You'll never be enough for him."

Her words sting, but they're true. "I know, I'm—"

"That doesn't mean there's anything wrong with you. He's the problem, not you. You're fucking great." She practically spits out the words. "Except now. You want to throw away what we have, as though it's nothing."

"It's future pain. That's what it is."

"Why are you so goddamn scared?"

"I'm being rational."

"You smile and act like you have this easy confidence, but underneath, you're still a scared little boy who's emotionally stunted. And I still want to be with you! Because I love you and you treat me well. Can't you accept that I love you, even if you're not ready to say it back? Can't you give us a chance?"

We stare at each other for a long, long time.

"No," I say at last. "I can't."

I TAKE the subway back downtown and go to Happy As Pie. The kitchen has always been a refuge of sorts for me. I get started on some cherry pie filling, but I can't focus.

I keep thinking about Josh.

I said words to him that I'd never expected to say to a man, and I'm angry at him for being unable to truly believe me. My love is not conditional on him being the perfect boyfriend.

Case in point? I still love him now, even though he broke up with me.

I'm furious at his father, too. I'm glad I talked back. I'm glad I swore in front of him. He deserved it. How can he not see what a great person Josh is? How can he not see how much damage he's done to his son?

I shove the container of cherry pie filling into the fridge and slam the door shut.

"Everything okay?" Fatima asks as she walks in.

It's only seven thirty in the morning and I've already had a break-up. This must be some kind of record.

"Yeah, everything's fine." I head to my office. "I'll be back out in a bit."

In my little office, I collapse on the chair and remember the time Josh found me here, doubled over with cramps, and brought me home and looked after me. He was so sweet.

And now he's gone.

I know he could love me, but I made my case and he turned me down.

God, if only I hadn't said those things about him being a distraction. Would he believe me if I'd kept my mouth shut the other day? If I hadn't seemed wary when I saw the jewelry box? I'm all in now, but I wasn't before...if only I'd gotten to this point sooner.

I shouldn't think about the what-ifs. It won't help anything.

I force myself to go over the bills. A while later, Ann knocks on the door.

"How was the party?" she asks.

"It was good," I say.

She raises her eyebrows. "Something's wrong."

Dammit. My face can't hide anything. "Josh broke up with me."

"Oh, sweetheart." She comes toward me and holds out her arms. "Can I hug you?"

I nod, and silent tears stream down my face as she comforts me. But I can't let myself fall apart too much at work.

I yearn for someone to take care of me, though. Just for a little while.

Despite our differences, I want my mother.

At five o'clock on Saturday, I leave Happy As Pie and head to the train station. My crew promises they can keep everything running smoothly on Sunday. It'll be the first time the shop opens without me. I trust them.

It's a two-hour train ride to London, Ontario and I try to

read. I have *Around the World with the CEO* and *Pregnant with the CEO's Twins* with me. I attempt the twins book first. The CEO is an Italian man who's the head of a big pharmaceutical company, and he has a one-night stand with a beautiful brunette he meets at a club. And then…surprise! She's pregnant! With twins! Which doesn't terrify me nearly as much as quintuplets.

Maybe I could have a baby or two. It wasn't something I let myself consider before, since I didn't plan to marry and being a single mother seemed incompatible with my career plans.

Now, though, I've had a relationship, and I start wondering…

I shut down that line of thinking. I won't let myself go there.

Eventually, I manage to lose myself in the book, and when we arrive in London, I'm more than halfway through it.

My father picks me up in the old car he's had since I was in high school. After I climb into the passenger's seat, he pats my shoulder and tells me it's good to see me, and we don't say much else on the half-hour drive to Ingleford. My dad has never been a big talker, except when trying to convince me that chocolate milk came from brown cows, and strawberry milk came from the rare pink cow.

When I step into my childhood home, a wonderful scent greets my nose.

My mother's chicken noodle soup.

"Sweetie, what happened?" Mom hurries into the front hall. "Why are you home?"

As soon as I see her, I lose it.

"He broke up with me," I say, sobbing into her shoulder.

I feel pathetic, crying over a man I didn't know for very long, but I can't help it.

She pulls back. "Josh? But I saw him on Monday. He was crazy about you. I could tell by the way he looked at you."

I sniffle. "I don't want to talk about it."

"That's okay, honey." She holds me for a moment, then ushers me into the kitchen and serves me a bowl of chicken soup. Rich broth and vegetables and egg noodles.

It's just what I need.

After dinner, she feeds me apple crisp and vanilla ice cream, and we watch TV for a while. When I crawl into bed, I finish *Pregnant with the CEO's Twins.*

Sunday morning, I wake up at six thirty, which is late for me. My parents are still asleep, so I go for a walk around Ingleford, the town I was so desperate to escape as a teenager. I walk by the grocery store, the convenience store, the diner, the Tim Hortons, the farmer's co-op, and the few other businesses that make up "downtown" Ingleford. None of them are open at this early hour. I walk by the elementary school that I attended for nine years. There's no high school—we were bussed to the next town. Aside from old Mr. Albert and his dog, I don't see anyone.

It's nice being back here for the weekend. Familiar. Comforting, in a way.

Though I never want to live here again.

When I get back to my parents' house, my mother is up.

"Want to make pancakes together?" she asks.

"Sure."

We've done this many times before, since I was a little girl. I sift together the dry ingredients and make a well in the center of the bowl. Then she pours in the milk and egg and melted butter and mixes it up while I heat up the pan. She scoops the batter into the pan, and I sprinkle on the blueberries—we always make blueberry pancakes in my family.

There's something I need to talk to my mom about while I'm here. I've been avoiding it for years, but I can't do that any longer, not when it haunts every conversation I have with her.

"Why did you tell me I'd fail?" I ask.

"What are you talking about?"

"When I told you, after I finished college, that I was staying in

Toronto and wanted to open my own place one day, you told me I wouldn't make it."

"I said that?" She frowns.

Jesus. She doesn't even remember. "You did. Those words have bothered me ever since. I want to know why my own mother thought I'd fail." I look at the blueberry pancakes in the pan rather than at her.

She takes a seat at the kitchen table. "I remember now. You were packing up everything in your bedroom, because you had no intention of coming back, except at holidays, and yes, I said some things. I didn't mean that, though."

I look up at her sharply. "You didn't mean it?"

"Of course not."

"Then why did you say it? Why have I spent the last decade determined to prove you wrong?"

"If it hadn't been for what I said, would you have stayed in Toronto?"

"Yes. But that made me angry. It motivated me." I flip over the pancakes.

She sighs. "I was afraid you *wouldn't* fail. In fact, I was pretty sure you'd succeed, and it scared me. Because I wanted, so badly, for you to live in Ingleford, or at least in London, so I could see you every week. At first, I imagined you being an accountant, but then I thought you could have a cute little bakery on Main Street —we could use one of those, don't you think?—with sandwiches and soups and cupcakes. I could stop in and see you whenever I wanted, and all my friends would be eating your baked goods. That was the sort of life I wanted for you. One that would keep you near me." She pauses. "All my other children are in the area. All my sisters are in the area. In our family, we stay. But you never wanted to stay, and selfishly, I didn't want you to have your dream. I'm sorry, honey. Truly. I now understand it's where you belong, and I'm proud of you."

"Thank you." I release a breath, trying to collect myself.

For a decade, I've wanted to prove my mother wrong, but I didn't need that extra motivation. I didn't start Happy As Pie just to prove a point; I started it because that was what I really, truly wanted.

After releasing another breath, I manage a smile as resentment seeps out of me.

I understand why she didn't want me to go. I miss my family, too.

I remove the pancakes from the pan and set the plate in front of my mother before pouring in batter for three more pancakes.

"I'll try to come back a little more often," I tell my mother.

"I'd like that. But, sweetheart, I'm so sorry I let you think that for so long. I had no idea."

"I forgive you." I pause. "I should have said something earlier."

"I understand why you didn't."

She pours a generous amount of maple syrup on her pancakes and starts eating, and all of a sudden, I imagine Josh as part of this family scene. I imagine us driving to Ingleford in his car, showing him the town where I grew up. The school, the diner, the ice cream parlor with its diverse mural. My childhood bedroom. I imagine sitting around the kitchen table in the morning, eating blueberry pancakes with him and my mom and dad. Dinner with my siblings and their children.

A sob escapes. I want that. I want that so much.

But it will never happen.

My mother walks over to me as I stand at the stove, watching the pancakes cook, and she puts her arms around me and holds me close. At last, I know she believes in me and she's proud of me, and it feels good to be in the kitchen with her and breathe in her Mom scent.

I just miss Josh so, so much.

$\approx$

When I get back to Toronto on Monday evening, I head straight home and eat the leftover chicken noodle soup that my mother sent with me. Afterward, I stare at the bottle of white wine that I bought last weekend, a bottle I thought I'd split with Josh.

Screw it.

I open the bottle and pour myself a glass, and I've just taken a sip when there's a knock on my door.

I freeze. I'm not expecting anyone.

But maybe it's Josh, and he changed his mind!

I fling open the door. It's not Josh, but Chloe and Valerie, and I try not to let my disappointment show. I'm happy to see my friends. I just...dammit, I wanted it to be Josh. Valerie is carrying two pie pans with my chocolate tart and berry crumble pie. Chloe is carrying what looks like two pints of ice cream, except there's nothing printed on the containers; they're plain white.

"Ann told us about Josh." Chloe puts down the pints and wraps her arms around me.

I let myself be embraced by Chloe, then Valerie.

"She also gave us extra pie to take to you," Valerie said. "Chloe brought ginger and taro ice cream that she made with our new equipment."

"We're going to have a little party. I see you've already got the wine." Chloe nods at my glass. "I'm so sorry, Sarah. I know you really like him."

We serve ourselves plates of pie and ice cream. The ice cream is really good. I'm impressed. As we eat and drink wine, I tell my friends about what happened with Josh, and I find myself crying for reasons other than the break-up.

I'm making friends in Toronto. My mother doesn't think I'll fail. Happy As Pie may not be a runaway success, but we're steadily building our business, and our first foray into catering went reasonably well.

Lots of things are coming together for me. It's wonderful, but I want to share it with Josh.

I don't regret telling him that I love him. It's the truth, and I'm glad he knows it, even if he doesn't know what to do with it.

I'm not sure I should have called him a scared little boy who's emotionally stunted, however. Josh is far from emotionally stunted. He knows how to care. He knows how to be a wonderful boyfriend. He just has some blind spots.

But I made my case. I didn't hold back. I don't think there's anything else I can do.

I sob around a bite of taro ice cream, and Chloe squeezes my shoulders.

Maybe one day I'll be able to love someone else the way I love Josh. Not anytime soon, though. I can't bear the thought of being with anyone but Josh Yu right now.

At least now I know that a relationship isn't something I have to avoid. It doesn't have to stop me from my dreams. And yes, opening myself up to someone and letting them into my life was scary, and yes, I got hurt, but it showed me that love is worth it.

We finish the bottle of wine, and Chloe jumps up to get another. I tell her which cupboard to look in, and in addition to the wine, she pulls out a box of Lucky Charms—yes, I keep my wine next to my cereal—and a Ziploc bag of Lucky Charms marshmallows.

Oh.

Oh.

"Why are there marshmallows in a separate bag?" she asks.

"I, um, bought a box, meticulously took out all the rainbows and unicorns and other marshmallows, and replaced them with… something else." My cheeks flame. "Then I swapped that 'special' box with the one in Josh's cupboard."

"What did you replace them with?" Valerie asks.

I tell my friends, and they burst into laughter.

For the first time since Pi Day, I really, truly laugh, too.

It'll take a while—probably a long, long while—but somehow, I'm going to be okay.

SOMETHING HITS me in the head.

Blearily, I open my eyes and lift my head from my desk. There's a Hazelnut Tech pen next to my hand and Amrita is standing at the door.

I check the clock. 6:15 pm. How long was I out?

"I can't believe you fell asleep at work," she says. "Tsk, tsk, setting such a poor example for your employees."

"I haven't been sleeping well lately." Last night, I managed four hours, and that was much better than the night before.

Amrita strides into the room and puts her hands on her hips. "You've been in a funk ever since the party, but the party went well. What aren't you telling me?"

"My dad isn't talking to me again."

"I thought things were better?"

"We had a heart-to-heart talk on Friday morning, but then Sarah came downstairs. He flipped out that I had a girl over and refused to believe she was my girlfriend and..." I shake my head. I don't want to talk about this, but I have to tell Amrita at some point. She's my closest friend. "And I broke up with Sarah."

"You broke up with Sarah?"

"Stop screaming. My head hurts."

"Why on earth did you break up with her?"

I gesture vaguely. "Because it'll never work out, and it's easier to end it now."

Though it's been far from easy. I was a mess all weekend, moping around my house, looking at pi napkins and pi tablecloths as I thought of her.

I didn't expect it would be anywhere near this bad, but in the past few weeks, Sarah has become an important part of my life. When we got a big client at work today, she was the person I most wanted to tell. But I didn't.

Amrita rolls her eyes. "What the hell is wrong with you?"

"She told me she loved me," I say morosely.

"Uh-huh. That scared the shit out of you?"

"Well, it was a bit soon."

"Do you love her back?"

I throw up my hands in frustration. "Why does that matter?"

"I don't know what *else* matters."

"It can't work, like I said."

"Why not?"

I sigh. "You know I don't do relationships."

"I didn't either, but then I met Holly." Amrita holds up her ring with a smile. "It just took the right person, and I think Sarah might be the right person for you."

"Who are you and what have you done with my best friend?"

I expect her to laugh, but she doesn't.

Instead, she walks over to me and grasps my shoulders. "If you don't get your head out of your ass, I'm going to *deliberately* pour hot ramen all over your crotch."

"Oh, for fuck's sake."

"Why, Josh? Why don't you think it will last?"

"Because love doesn't last for me."

"You had one relationship before Sarah came along, and that

was in high school, and… Oh. I get it. This is about your daddy issues, isn't it?"

"I don't have *daddy issues*," I protest.

"Mm-hmm. Whatever you say."

"You're infuriating when you use that tone, did you know that?"

She just stands there, arms crossed. "Mm-hmm. Whatever you say."

"Amrita!"

"You think your father doesn't love you—and I understand why, given his actions—so you don't see how anyone else could keep loving you, either, and you still haven't forgiven yourself for what happened when you were a teenager. But the giant rift between you and your father is on him, not you. I've seen how hard you try to make him proud, your efforts to talk to him. You threw a goddamn Pi Day party to entice him to come to Toronto." She takes a deep breath. "You need to let this go. It's frustrating to see how your self-worth and your ability to accept love is tied to your father, and he's shown over and over that he's not worthy of you."

"But he's my father, and he's a decent person. Really, he is. If Sarah hadn't slept over…"

"You're thirty-three years old. There is nothing wrong with having your girlfriend sleep in your own house."

"Except my parents were there. And they didn't know she was my girlfriend."

Amrita sighs. "You have to stop letting him have so much of an invisible presence in your life. You need to make room for other people. Beneath the easy confidence you project much of the time, you're vulnerable."

"You sound like Sarah."

"Because we're both smart women."

I pick up the pen Amrita threw at me and toss it at her. She catches it easily.

"Let's go out for beers," she says.

"Now you're talking."

"And you can help me plan my wedding."

"Um…"

"Just kidding! Man, you should see the look on your face. Will you be in the wedding party, though? Plan me a nice bachelorette party?"

"Of course," I say with a smile.

I will absolutely do that for Amrita.

It's Tuesday after work, and a pot of beef stew is simmering on the stove. I made it to give me some connection to Sarah, to remind me of the night I cooked for her.

I miss her so much.

But this will go away soon, won't it?

It can't last much longer, right?

Unfortunately, I'm starting to fear that might not be true.

It doesn't have to be like this! says a voice inside my head, which sounds suspiciously like Amrita.

I don't know. Amrita is just high on love because she recently got engaged.

There are a couple of reports I need to read, a few e-mails to respond to, so I pick up my laptop as I wait for the stew to cook.

Ten minutes later, I give up. I can't concentrate and I have zero motivation, which isn't like me at all. I'm usually driven. That's how I got where I am in life.

How much did that have to do with trying to make my father proud? Would Hazelnut Tech have been as successful if I hadn't been determined to mend the rift with my father?

I'm not sure, but I'm happy with my professional life. I don't wish I'd done things differently.

I close the laptop. Perhaps I need a vacation. Sitting on a

beach in the Caribbean with Sarah—now that would be a good way to spend a week.

Except I broke up with Sarah, and that's the reason I'm down in the dumps. Also my father, but in truth, it's her more than anything.

I miss her so much, but this is the way it has to be.

The doorbell rings four times in a row.

Goddammit, I heard you the first time.

I stalk to the door, ready to give the person who's trying to sell me duct or window cleaning a piece of my mind.

But when I thrust open the door, I'm too stunned to speak.

My mother is standing on my front porch, her purse in one hand, the handle of a rolling suitcase clutched in the other. Her expression is blazing.

Great. Just what I need. Another woman who's pissed off at me.

Still, I instinctively flip into Good Son mode and grab her suitcase and usher her inside. "Did you drive all the way from Ottawa?" I can't imagine it. My mother hates driving long distances.

She shakes her head. "I took the train."

"With Dad?"

"That idiot? No!" She utters some choice words in Cantonese about my father.

My eyes bug out of my head. I've never heard her speak like this before.

She takes off her boots, marches into the living room, and plants herself on my sofa. "I'm staying with you now." She doesn't ask; she just says it's happening.

"For how long?"

"Until he apologizes!"

"For what?" I'm vibrating with rage. What did Dad do to her?

"Don't be stupid. You know what for. Until he talks to you again."

I breathe out a sigh of relief. That's all it is. Good. "I think you'll be waiting a while."

"I don't care. I refuse to go back until that donkey-brained numbskull treats you with respect!"

I attempt to suppress a laugh, but it sneaks out anyway.

"Joshua!"

"I'm sorry. I never thought I'd see the day when you'd call anyone—least of all Dad—a donkey-brained numbskull."

"Well, it's the new me."

I admit, I'm a bit terrified.

"He treats me like a delicate blossom, always saying I shouldn't trouble myself with this or that or I'll make myself sicker, but I've been cancer-free for over a decade. I will not put up with this stupid coddling any longer. I will not ignore the way he's treating you. I should have put my foot down a long time ago." She stomps her foot to emphasize her point.

I'm not sure what to say. A part of me is glad she's taken my side so decisively, but I'm afraid I will now have my mother living with me for the rest of her life, and that isn't something I was quite prepared for, not at this point in time.

"Are you hungry?" I ask. "I made beef stew." I gesture for her to follow me into the kitchen, where I ladle out two bowls of stew and cut some of the baguette I bought on the way home.

"So fancy! Like you knew I was coming." Her gaze is caught by something on the fridge. "Melinda is getting married? And she invited you?"

Ugh. I'd left the invitation on the fridge to remind me to ask Sarah if she'd be my date.

Well, that's not happening now.

"I saw her on the news the other day," Mom says, "talking about the changes to the sex-ed curriculum. She is so well-spoken. I used to think maybe you would get back together and marry her one day."

"I don't feel that way about Melinda anymore. I haven't for a long time." It's hard to believe my mother actually wanted that to happen. Dad would have been furious—a reminder of what happened when I was a teenager.

"I know, I know. You have Sarah now!"

I start to protest, but she continues talking before I can get a word in.

"I think we failed you in some ways," she says. "Focusing on school, going to a good university. We did not think about the reality of high school. Drugs, sex, rock 'n' roll."

"Um…"

"We should have had proper talks with you about these things."

"About rock music?"

"Ah, don't silly! You know what I mean. Peer pressure, safe sex. Should not have left it all to the school."

"We did learn about those things in school, but… Can we not have this conversation?"

"I want to ask about Sarah! I'm very happy for you. I knew that one day, you would get over this bachelor lifestyle and find a woman." Mom tries a bite of the stew. "Mm, this is delicious. Did she teach you how to make it?"

I shake my head. "Sarah and I broke up."

"What? I just saw you on Friday. Is it because of your father? Aiyah! He is a donkey-brained numbskull, scaring off your girl-friend. I know, he said it was tacky, probably made her feel like a cheap whore, and she decided she wanted nothing to do with your family."

I can't get used to the way my mother is talking today—she's so different when it's just the two of us. I guess Dad cast a long shadow over all of my interactions with her. She's angry, but she's also lively. It's nice in a way, even if I'm scrambling to keep up.

"Sarah didn't dump me," I say. "I broke up with her."

"Why?"

I shake my head again.

Mom throws a piece of bread at me. "Fine, don't tell me, I'll get answers out of you later. I expect I'll be staying here for a while. But I want you to know: I don't care that she's white. We already went through it with Nancy, and it was an adjustment, yes, but no problem."

I pinch the bridge of my nose. "Mom, can we not talk about Sarah for a while?"

"Fine, fine."

We watch a Cantonese drama after dinner, and my mother gets annoyed with me when we have to turn on the English subtitles because I can't quite catch everything.

Afterward, I make up the guest room for her, and then I go to bed and stare at the ceiling for a long time, which is my usual bedtime routine these days.

When I get home from work on Wednesday, my mom serves me winter melon soup and we talk about my day at work. It's nice to have her here. I'm sure I'll get sick of having her around soon enough, but for now, I prefer it to being alone, with only Sarah to occupy my thoughts.

"Why did you break up with Sarah?" Mom asks.

Great. I bet she'll ask me every day until I give a satisfactory answer.

I have to tell her something, but what pops out of my mouth is a surprise.

"I don't deserve it."

I didn't realize it until I spoke the words, but that's the reason. After Sarah and I spent our first night together, I realized I'd been holding myself back from relationships in part because I felt like I didn't deserve it. But then I started telling myself that wasn't true, until the argument with my father made me feel otherwise.

"Why not?" Mom demands. "Nice young man like you, of course you deserve it!" She pauses. "Ah, I understand. Your father won't talk to you, so you still haven't forgiven yourself for being a foolish teenager. But he is a donkey-brained numbskull—no need to pay attention to him."

"He's your husband."

She shrugs. "For now."

"What? Are you thinking of getting a divorce?"

The thought seems almost scandalous. None of their friends are divorced.

"I hope not," she says, "but look how much he has messed you up, and he's gotten in the way of our relationship, too." She gestures between us. "Because of him, you only come home at Christmas, and I don't blame you. And it's hard for me to come to Toronto because I don't like driving far. He is haunting every conversation between us, but I won't let him, not anymore."

She drops her soup spoon and puts her hand on mine, and I'm trying not to cry, but I will eventually lose the battle.

Now that I've heard it not just from Amrita, but from my mother, I understand it's true. I haven't forgiven myself. And since I haven't forgiven myself, I couldn't sincerely believe I deserved it, and one conversation with my father was enough for me to back away from what I had with Sarah.

Because of what happened when we were younger, Melinda became a sex-ed crusader who encourages parents—especially in the Chinese community—to have the difficult conversations, even if it's taboo. In many ways, the incident was far worse for her, and yes, it affected who she became, but it hasn't stopped her from living her life. She hasn't let it.

I have.

It's not true that love won't last for me. My mother may have been disappointed in me many times, but her love was never conditional, even if she rarely spoke of it. I have a good relationship with my sisters. With Amrita, who loves me in a platonic way, even when I'm being an idiot and she throws chopsticks and pens at my head. I've known her for over a decade and we built a business together…and we're still close.

Sarah is nothing like my father, and it's not true that I know nothing about love. A different kind of love, but still.

I love Sarah.

I love every single part of her, and the time we spent together was like nothing else I've ever experienced.

I want her back.

But first I have to forgive myself, and I can do that now.

I forgive myself for not meeting all of my father's expectations when I was young. Like many teenagers, I had sex. I tried drugs. I skipped class. I wasn't a model student like my sisters; I wasn't exactly who my father wanted me to be. But that doesn't make me a bad person.

I'm happy with who I am today, and the journey that led me to Sarah Winters.

"I do deserve it."

"Finally," Mom says. "You are showing how smart you are!"

I chuckle and spoon more soup into my mouth. As I swallow, a strange sense of freedom spreads through my body.

Freedom from my father. Freedom from the past.

I won't let the past stop me from moving forward. I will allow myself to love a woman who wiped butter tart filling from my lips before she knew my name, a woman who accidentally stabbed me with a fork. A woman who is sexy and ambitious and can make incredible pie.

Speaking of pie, I smell something other than winter melon soup in the kitchen. Sure enough, butter tarts are cooling on a rack on the counter.

When Mom sees where I'm looking, she stands up and piles some tarts on a plate for me.

"I don't know why I made these," she says. "You have a terrible diet and I should not be encouraging it."

"What do you mean I have a terrible diet?"

She opens a cupboard and pulls out a box of Lucky Charms. "You're thirty-three years old and you eat this? It was a treat on Sundays when you were a kid, but why is a grown man eating multi-colored marshmallows for breakfast?"

I recall the first morning I spent with Sarah. I told her that CEOs always eat Lucky Charms for breakfast.

Ha. I smile.

I don't have to keep missing Sarah. I can go to her right now. I hope she'll forgive me. I hope she'll say we can be together, no matter how much I screwed up in the past week.

I still have some lingering fears, but they're overwhelmed by my love for her, and as she said, we can learn how to do this together. She told me about her own fears, how she felt vulnerable, but she didn't run away because of them.

I'm determined to be the man she deserves.

Mom pours herself a bowl of Lucky Charms and soy milk.

"You scolded me for having Lucky Charms," I say, "and now you're eating some?"

"That's the main reason I let you eat them as a kid. An excuse to buy them, so I could have some, too."

I chuckle as I stare at my mother's bowl of cereal. Something is very wrong with these Lucky Charms. Where are the colors? Is this a defective box that didn't get the marshmallows?

I am outraged, I tell you. Outraged!

Then I realize that there actually *are* marshmallows, but they're similar in color to the cereal, and they're shaped like...penises?

My mom jerks away from the box as though it's a giant spider. "This isn't Lucky Charms. Did you buy some cheap knock-off at the Chinese mall?" She squints. "It's X-rated cereal!"

I laugh. I can't help it. I laugh and laugh.

I know Sarah did this, probably when she was here for Pi Day —I haven't had Lucky Charms since then. I'm sure she never envisioned me discovering the penis marshmallows like *this*.

I love that woman.

"Mom, I'm sorry, but I've got something important to do. I have to leave and—"

Just then, there's a pounding on the door, followed by five rings of the doorbell. I hurry to the door, convinced it's Sarah, convinced she must have somehow known exactly when I was going to change my mind.

But that's not who greets me.

"Where is your mother?" Dad stomps in, not even bothering to remove his boots. "She's here, isn't she?"

I'm not surprised to see him. One thing I know about my dad is that even though he's a giant jackass to me, he loves my mother.

"Answer me!" he says.

"So many years of refusing to speak to me, and now you're demanding I answer your questions?" I can't help it.

He glares at me. "Stop being such a smart-mouth."

"You know, Mom left because she's angry with how you treat me, so maybe you want to start by changing that."

"I'm talking to you now, like she wanted."

"Aiyah!" Mom comes into the front hall. "This is not what I meant by talking. You apologize!"

"You had no right to leave and make me drive halfway across the province," Dad says. "You know how worried I was? You wouldn't even pick up your phone."

"You have to stop treating me like I'm a fragile, sick child."

"Anything could have happened to you."

I stand there for a minute as their argument switches to Cantonese. My father wants my mother to come home, but he also seems uninterested in having a proper conversation with me.

I take a deep breath. His rejection still affects me, but not nearly as much as before.

My self-worth shouldn't depend on a man whose actions have hurt me so much over the years. Yes, he's my father, but I don't need his approval. I am a good person even without it, and I won't let him have so much power over me.

I'm free.

I hurry to the kitchen to gather a few things, then come back and put on my shoes and jacket. "Sorry, I have somewhere else to be."

My parents ignore me and continue to argue.

I slip out the door, jump in my car, and start driving.

"I'M GOING to be okay. I'm going to be okay."

I repeat the words to myself as I putter around the kitchen at Happy As Pie on Wednesday evening. A few more minutes of cleaning up and then I'll head home. I usually would have left by now, but I was experimenting with a few things.

I'm starting to feel at home in the kitchen again. I couldn't lose myself in my work right after Josh broke up with me, and he's still on my mind nearly all the time. But somehow, I make it through each day.

Next month, I have a small catering gig with a tech company that heard about us from one of Josh's employees. Slowly, I'm building the business I dreamed of.

I'm taking off my apron when someone knocks on the back door. Cautiously, I open it, and my heart hammers when I see who it is.

"Josh," I whisper.

He doesn't have the kind and friendly expression that he wore the day I met him.

Instead, he looks serious and determined.

He sets something aside on the counter and takes my hands in his, and then he says something completely unexpected.

"I found the marshmallow dicks."

It takes me a moment to figure out what he's talking about.

The Lucky Charms.

"Unfortunately," he says, "my mother was there at the time."

My cheeks heat. God, I keep screwing things up with his parents. "I'm sorry, I—"

"It's okay." He raises one hand and caresses my cheek. "I love that you painstakingly removed the colorful marshmallows. I love that you make the best pie in the world and are committed to your business. I love the way you savor good food. I love the way you kiss. I love the way you told me you love me...even though that was scary for you, just like it's scary for me, but I'm still going to say it." He pauses. "I love you."

I pinch myself to make sure this is real.

It's real, alright.

"I'm sorry I couldn't accept your feelings for me. God, Sarah, I'm so sorry. It freaked me out, and I was afraid you'd snatch it away at any moment. I couldn't look beyond what had happened with my father—I couldn't see that all the other relationships in my life are nothing like that one. But now I know that your love isn't conditional on me being perfect. If you'll give me another chance, I want to spend every hour of every day proving that I love you. And I know how much Happy As Pie means to you, and I promise I won't get in the way of that—I want to support you in every way I can. I want to wake up early so I can make coffee for you before you go to the bakery and maybe even convince you to eat Lucky Charms. I want to bring you soup and a hot water bottle when you need it and rub your feet after a long day of work. I want so much with you, and I can't promise I'll do it all perfectly, but I promise to do my best and love you as you deserve."

I blink back tears and smile at him.

He's here, and he wants to be with me again, and he's willing to give me so much.

A month ago, I never could have imagined this happening. I was determined to focus on my pie shop and nothing else, but now I see that with Josh, my life can be even better. I can hear the sincerity in every word he says, and there's no way I'd turn him down.

"Yes," I say, softly at first. Then I repeat it. Louder. "Yes."

He smiles at me, even more radiant than his usual smiles—and those are pretty freaking awesome. But now, he's smiling as though he's just been given everything he ever desired.

He takes a box out of his pocket, identical to the jewelry box that contained the pi necklace. "I got this one first, but I chickened out. I couldn't give it to you even though it represented the feelings I felt for you, the ones that scared me and that I refused to articulate. So, I bought the other necklace, too."

I grasp the pi pendant, which had slipped behind my T-shirt, and hold it up. Yes, I'm wearing it today, even though he'd broken up with me. I couldn't help it; I wanted some part of him near me, despite fearing he was gone from my life forever.

But now he's back.

He opens up the jewelry box to reveal a white gold necklace with a double heart pendant, one of the hearts lined with tiny crystals.

"I love it," I whisper.

"May I?" He takes it out of the box and undoes the clasp.

"Of course."

He places the necklace around my neck, and a frisson of energy runs through me when he touches the back of my neck and fastens the clasp. He moves to take the other necklace off, but I stop him.

"I want to keep them both on for now. I love the pi one, too. A symbol of how we got to where we are now."

And then, at long last, he kisses me. His lips descend to mine, and at first, it's a tender, loving kiss, but as he wraps his arms around me, it becomes more frantic. Passionate. He cups his hands under my ass and scoops me up. He walks over to the nearest counter, and I know he has every intention of making love to me in the kitchen. I run my hands up under his Henley, and he groans as I scrape my nails over his bare skin.

"I...can't." It's a struggle to get out that word, as he's grabbing my breast and circling his thumb over my nipple. "There's no way I'm having sex in my kitchen. It's unsanitary."

He barks out a laugh that reverberates in my chest. "Your office, then."

"No, I want to do this properly."

"I'm having decidedly *im*proper thoughts about you right now."

 "My apartment isn't all that far..."

The next thing I know, he's bundling me into my winter coat and leading me out the door, and we hold hands as we hurry home.

We strip each other bare in record time, and finally, there's nothing between us. When he enters me, I hiss out a breath of pleasure and feel as though everything, *everything* is just right.

～

After we make love—twice—we cuddle up in bed. I touch the necklaces around my neck, the only things I'm still wearing.

"I'll be right back," Josh says.

I miss his body heat, but he isn't gone long. When he returns, he presents me with a plastic container containing two butter tarts.

I give him a mock glare. "These were made by someone other than me. How dare you!"

"My mother baked them."

"Well, in that case..." I take one out of the container. It is, indeed, a delicious butter tart.

"She showed up at my house yesterday, saying she wouldn't go home until my father started talking to me again and treating me with respect. He showed up today, and that's when I left, but..." Josh blows out a breath. "I'm not sure he has any intention of having a real relationship with me, one that won't disappear the instant I do something he doesn't approve of, but I guess I can accept that."

My heart aches for Josh. He doesn't deserve this.

"But I won't let him cast a shadow over the rest of my life anymore, including my relationships with everyone else in my family."

As we nibble on our butter tarts, we catch up on everything that has happened since Pi Day. I tell him about my trip to Ingleford and my conversation with my mother.

We're just finishing our tarts when Josh's phone buzzes from inside his discarded pants. He ignores it, but then it buzzes again.

"Go ahead and check it," I say. "There's something I want to get from the kitchen."

I head out of my bedroom in the nude and grab the bag of Lucky Charms marshmallows from the top cupboard. When I climb back into bed, Josh is still looking at his phone. Wordlessly, he shows me a text message.

Dear Josh, it's your father. I have stolen (I mean, borrowed) your mother's phone so I can send my first text message. I'm sorry. I really am sorry for everything, and I'm not just saying that so your mother will come home. Please come back tonight so we can talk for real, and I promise I won't judge you for all the things I judged you for before. We will start again. I miss my son. Love, Dad.

I know how much this means to Josh. He may have let go of his desperation for his father's approval, of feeling unworthy because his dad wouldn't talk to him. But he still wants a relationship with him.

"Do you want to go now?" I ask.

Josh wraps his arms around me and kisses my cheek. "No, it's late, and there's nowhere I'd rather be than here with you. There will be plenty of time for that tomorrow. Just a minute." He taps out a message, then puts his phone down. "Tonight, I'm all yours." He kisses me again.

I never knew how much feeling a kiss could convey until I met Josh.

"I don't know a lot about being anyone's boyfriend," he says. "I'm woefully out of practice, but like I said, I promise to do my very best with you."

"You're doing a great job so far. I'm not very familiar with what it's like to be someone's girlfriend, either, but I will be here whenever you need me, putting marshmallow dicks in your Lucky Charms." I take out the bag of the real Lucky Charm marshmallows, which I'd hidden under the blankets. "Look what I have."

He laughs. "Do these offend your fancy foodie tastes?"

"Maybe a little, but if you like them, I don't care. And seriously, how could anyone hate a marshmallow unicorn?"

But instead of the unicorn, I pull out a little marshmallow heart and pop it in his mouth, and then I feed myself a green clover.

I feel very, very lucky right now.

Everything is coming together in my life, and I know the road ahead won't be perfect, but Josh and I will be on it together.

Once upon a time, a handsome CEO walked into my pie shop and asked me to cater a Pi Day party, and I stabbed him in the arm with a fork, and somehow, we fell in love. We discovered we could be amazing together, like chocolate and hazelnuts. Even though neither of us thought we wanted romance and love, we found them with each other.

I clutch the pi and heart pendants in my hand and press a kiss to Josh's lips.

I am, indeed, happy as pie.

It's Easter Sunday and we're having dim sum.

Although my family isn't Christian, we always did something for Easter, and in recent years, my sisters would go to a restaurant in Ottawa with my parents. Not me, though.

But this year, they all came to Toronto, and there are twelve of us seated around the table. Mom and Dad, Nancy and Wendy and their families, and me and Sarah.

Sarah squeezes my leg under the table and rotates the lazy Susan to get herself some turnip cake, which, for mysterious reasons, she enjoys. I place my hand over hers and smile.

A few months ago, I never would have imagined this happening. Me and a girlfriend at a family meal. I have a *girlfriend*, and she makes my heart sing whenever I look at her. And while I might have imagined eating dim sum with my sisters and parents, a part of me feared I'd never have a real conversation with my father again, no matter how hard I tried.

Yet here we are.

Things with my father still aren't perfect, but they're better than before. I hope we'll continue to get along, but regardless, I won't let him get in my head and make me feel bad about myself.

My parents' relationship is on slightly shaky ground. My mother has a lot of resentment over how my father treated me over the years, plus resentment over the things he's done that have supposedly been for her health. They've started couples therapy. I was surprised Dad wasn't too proud to go to therapy, but he doesn't want to lose his wife, and he's determined to change.

Mom loves Sarah and convinced her to share her recipe for chocolate hazelnut tarts, which, to be honest, I didn't think Sarah would ever give to anyone, but she has.

"Number Nineteen," Wendy says, "please stop hogging the siu mai."

I put the bamboo steamer back on the lazy Susan. "You have to stop calling me that."

"Am confused," Dad says. "Why do you call him Number Nineteen?"

I sigh. "Because I was number nineteen on a list of eligible bachelors in Toronto." I turn to Wendy. "But you can't call me that anymore, because even though I'm not married, I'm very much taken."

I wink at Sarah, and she smiles back at me. It's pretty wonderful, what we have.

When we're almost done eating, my father gets up. It looks like he's trying to be sneaky about it, but my father is a big man, and it's not easy for him to sneak out of the back corner.

"Oh, no, you don't," Nancy says, pushing back her chair so he can't get through.

Dad looks at me. "What about you? Are you going to try to stop me?"

I cross my arms and lean back in my chair. "Nah, go ahead. You're just going to the washroom, right?"

"For a CEO," Nancy says, "you're pretty stupid. He's obviously trying to pay the bill."

Wendy shrugs. "Whatever, the bill has already been paid. He's too late."

"What?" Nancy cries. "Is that what you were doing when you took Lindy to the washroom? Using your children to help you pay the bill—that's low."

"That's when I tried to give them my credit card," Wendy says. "But they refused, saying they already had one on file."

Everyone turns to me. I shrug innocently.

"Wah, how could you?" Dad pulls some bills out of his wallet and tries to hand them across the table.

"You're making a scene. The meal isn't even over yet." Mom pulls back his arm.

He returns the money to his wallet and frowns. "Where is my credit card? And the rest of my money? I only have forty bucks!"

Now it's my mother's turn to shrug innocently.

"You did this?" Dad asks. "You managed to steal my wallet when I wasn't looking?"

Mom holds up a credit card and a wad of bills and shrugs again.

He grabs the money and card back. "So sneaky."

"Let the children pay sometimes," she says.

"Fine, fine," he grumbles, putting everything back in his wallet. A moment later, he and my mother share a private grin.

I touch Sarah's hand and smile.

Sarah and I are cozied up in the twin bed in her old room at her parents' house. It's a tight squeeze, but there's nowhere else I'd rather be. Finally, after dim sum with my family and dinner in Ingleford with her family, I get to be all alone with her and hold her in my arms.

She rests her head on my chest and yawns. "It's been a long day."

"It has, though you woke up two hours later than usual." Sarah closed Happy As Pie for the Easter weekend.

"True, but there was some vigorous love-making before I even got out of bed."

"Such a hardship."

She laughs and kisses my chin. "And so much food. I won't need to eat for a week."

"Same here."

Tomorrow morning, Sarah will take me on a tour of the town. Her life is in Toronto now, but this is where she spent the first eighteen years of her life, and I want to know everything about her.

I already know so much. Like how freaking delicious all the food she makes is. Like the face she makes when she's trying to work out a new recipe...and the face she makes when I slide inside her. I know there's a freckle on the back of her left earlobe, and a small scar from a burn on the inside of her right wrist. I know she's beautiful and driven; I know she will make things happen. Even when they don't work out as planned, I will be there beside her.

I will always be there.

Because Sarah Winters is the best thing that ever happened to me. And I know I'm worthy of her affection, despite my flaws, and I'm not afraid of what we have, not anymore.

In two weeks, she'll accompany me to Melinda's wedding, and at the end of the summer, to Amrita and Holly's wedding. The following summer, maybe our own wedding?

I know it's early, but I'm already thinking about it.

But for now, I push those thoughts aside and focus on being in the moment with Sarah, who's pulling my shirt over my head. I take off hers, and we lie together, skin against skin.

"I love you, sweetheart," I murmur, cuddling closer, "and not just because you make the world's best pear ginger crumble pie."

She brought two for dinner, and despite all the food I'd eaten, I had seconds and was tempted to have thirds.

"Love you, too," she says, "and not just because you brought me breakfast in bed this morning."

I made her Hong Kong-style French toast—I'm becoming more adept in the kitchen—and a mug of coffee with two heart-shaped marshmallows, from the Lucky Charms box, of course.

"Or because of all those orgasms," she adds. "Though they were pretty spectacular."

"Mm, I could tell by the noises you made." I turn out the light and kiss her cheek. "Goodnight, darling."

Tomorrow will be another day I get to spend with Sarah, and I can't wait.

ACKNOWLEDGMENTS

Thank you to my editor, Latoya C. Smith, for helping me make this book the best it could be, and thank you to Flirtation Designs for the lovely cover!

To write this story, I had to do a little research on pies and running a bakery. (Not a hardship, I promise.) I want to thank Janelle at The Pie Commission and Vanessa at The Rolling Pin for answering my questions.

Thank you also to Toronto Romance Writers, as well as my husband and father, for all your support.

Jackie Lau decided she wanted to be a writer when she was in grade two, sometime between writing "The Heart That Got Lost" and "The Land of Shapes." She later studied engineering and worked as a geophysicist before turning to writing romance novels. Jackie lives in Toronto with her husband, and despite living in Canada her whole life, she hates winter. When she's not writing, she enjoys gelato, gourmet donuts, cooking, hiking, and reading on the balcony when it's raining.

To learn more and sign up for her newsletter, visit jackielaubooks.com.

CPSIA information can be obtained
at www.ICGtesting.com
Printed in the USA
LVHW011510200819
628308LV00003B/340/P

9 781775 304791